Rules Worth Breaking

A FOUND FAMILY ROCK ROMANCE

ELLE WHITTAKER

LEMONADE
HEART
PRESS

ISBN (print): 979-8-9909996-5-7

ISBN (e-book): 979-8-9909996-6-4

Cover Design by Mitxeran

Content Guide

This book contains adult language/profanity, people confidently owning their desire, and consensual open-door sex scenes.

Contents

QUEEN ANNE

Marlowe Wainscoate
Guitar, backup vocals. Blue eyes, brown hair. Rebel, lover
of weird walks.

Jem Reed
Lead vocals. Militaristic, and known for her killer
performances and full sleeve tattoos. Half red, half blonde
mullet.

Rose Devangelo
Bass. Quiet and caring. Level-headed, short brown
pixie cut.

Ducky Roberts
Drums. Chaotic and funny. Purple hair and lots of
piercings.

THE BOY SCOUTS OF ATLANTIS

SIMON BOROUGHS
Guitar, lead vocals. Rule follower and photographer of venue bathrooms.

WENDY JONES
Drums. Victorian changeling boy who turns feral on the drums.

FELIX CHRISTOPOLOUS
Keys. Emo kid. Grumpy black cat in both energy and appearance.

AARON TRUVEAU
Bass. Golden retriever himbo. All-American blonde Clark Kent, a little gullible.

"Guttermouth" by Bree Sharp
"Entertain" by Sleater-Kinney
"Berlin" by Black Rebel Motorcycle Club
"Excuse Me Mr" by No Doubt
"Shut Up Kiss Me" by Angel Olsen
"The Devil is an Angel" by Jackson+Sellers
"Bathroom Floor" by Queenadilla
"Evil and a Heathen" by Franz Ferdinand
"See Through Head" by The Hives
"Mind Reader" by Silverchair
"Last Nite" by The Strokes
"Fell In Love With a Girl" by The White Stripes
"Shine A Little Light" by The Black Keys
"Private Idaho" by The B-52's
"Can You Picture That" by Dr. Teeth & The Electric Mayhem
"Kiss Me" by Sixpence None The Richer
"Make Me Feel" by Janelle Monae
"Take a Walk" by Raphael Saddiq
"In the Moonlight" by Pearl Jam
"Let's Get It On" by Marvin Gaye
"My Sweet Lady" by John Denver

*This book is a love letter not just to spicy, romantic love, but also to
the deep love that takes place within friendships, and to the deep love
of music that so many of us carry.*

*Romance and friendship and music may be different kinds of love, but
their depth can be the same.*

Prologue

April 6: Berkley, California

Marlowe

Ducky leaned over and shouted in my ear. "Why do I want to fuck every guitarist with good hair?" she asked.

I grinned, then glanced up at the band onstage. "Is it something about their fingers?" I asked.

"No," Ducky replied. "I think it's the hair."

Ducky did have a point. The guitarist on stage did have really good hair…wavy and long enough to get into his eyes in an angsty poet kind of way. He was moving his head up and down as he played, staring at the floor. I looked over and noticed Ducky biting her lip. I laughed.

"We shouldn't wait up for you tonight, should we?" I asked.

"I sure hope not," Ducky replied, her eyes still on the stage. The band finished their song and Ducky screamed louder than the rest of the people around us.

"I'm gonna go get another drink," I shouted. But

1

Ducky probably wasn't even listening. She was piling her bright purple hair into a bun on the top of her head, revealing her undercut, and walking purposefully toward the stage.

At the bar, I leaned over and asked for another Shirley Temple.

"Hey, I think you dropped this," a low voice said next to me.

I turned and then forgot how to breathe. Because the man standing next to me was the hottest man I had ever seen in my life.

He was well built, but not in an obnoxious way. Just in the way that made you want to know what it felt like to have him put his arms around you and squeeze. Striking green eyes. Curly brown hair that went just past his shoulders, looking so soft that I had to clench my fingers to stop from reaching out to touch it. The man was holding out a guitar pick. It took me a moment to realize that it was one of mine. The one I'd thrown out to the crowd during our set earlier.

"You can keep it," I managed.

The man raised one eyebrow. "What do I have to do in return?" His voice carried just a hint of meaning—not so much that I could be absolutely sure he was flirting with me, but enough that it was a possibility.

If I was a cooler girl, I would come up with some kind of flirty, hot thing to say in return. But at the moment, my brain was complete static. Because I had just noticed his hands and how were his hands also hot?

"You have to…um…tell me your name," I said.

The man grinned, then said, "I'm Simon."

It took me a full five seconds to realize that I was staring, open-mouthed, practically drooling. It wasn't until Simon raised his eyebrows at me that I remembered to reply. "Marlowe," I replied. The band onstage had started playing another song, and the room had gotten loud again.

"What was that?" the man asked, leaning forward.

Oh god. He smelled so good. Citrus and spice and *guy*.

"I'm Marlowe," I repeated into Simon's ear. I resisted the urge to reach out to touch his bicep as I spoke, because then I might not want to let go, and we just barely met.

He straightened to smile down at me. "Nice to meet you," he said."I liked your set."

"Thank," I replied. "I mean thank you. Thanks."

Simon smiled at me, and I was trying to think of something else to say, but before I could form a complete sentence in my mind, Jem appeared at my elbow.

"Have you seen Rose?" she asked.

"No, why?"

Jem shook her head. "The next band's keyboardist wanted to talk to her about something."

"Speaking of which," Simon said.

And then he walked away.

Which gave me a great view, and also made me very sad.

"Who was that?" Jem asked.

"Simon," I said.

"Who?"

"That's literally all I know."

But within five minutes, I learned that he was the lead guitarist and singer of the Boy Scouts of Atlantis, the third band playing tonight.

And that he was really really really good.

At both singing and playing guitar.

The Boy Scouts of Atlantis had this huge theatrical sound, even though it was just four guys up there. It was guitar, bass, drums, and keys, but they managed to sound like a combination of Bowie and Silverchair and Franz

Ferdinand. It was sexy and big and they made me feel the music in my bones.

After their first song ended, Simon spoke into the microphone. "Thanks to West Grand Music Hall for having us tonight. And special thanks to Marlowe, the guitarist from Queen Anne, for the use of her guitar pick." He held his hand up, my pick held between his fingers.

And all of that, for some reason, made me want to take my pants off and climb up onto the stage. Was I ovulating? What the hell.

"This next song is called 'Too Light for Bats.' Two, three, four!"

They launched into their next song, and I spent the next fifteen minutes trying not to stare at Simon's hands. Or his lips. Or his hair.

It's not just that Simon was attractive because of his hands and his lips and his hair. It was also because of the way he held his guitar. The way he moved his hips. The contortions of his body when he solo'd. There were moments when I couldn't figure out where to look—at his fingers moving over the frets or his lips pressed close to the mic or the beads of sweat that moved down his temples, making his hair curl tighter. There was one song when he screamed into the mic and his jawline was somehow hypnotic.

At one point, he held his guitar out to the audience to play, and I saw him mouth "sorry" to the sound engineer in back, and even *that* was attractive.

It wasn't until their last song that the pieces fell into place. "That's Aaron on the bass, Wendy Jones on the drums, Felix on the keys, and I'm Simon, and we are the Boy Scouts of Atlantis!"

I turned to Jem. "Wait, is that Rose's Felix?"

"I mean, he doesn't belong to Rose, but yeah, they went to high school together," Jem replied.

"She didn't tell us they were so good!"

But Jem was looking thoughtfully up at the band. "We should play more shows with them," she said.

I glanced up at Simon again. "Yeah, we should," I replied.

CHAPTER 1

You Don't Need to Yell

JULY 5: PETALUMA, CALIFORNIA

MARLOWE

"Ugh, why do drums take up so much room?" I groaned. I stared at the back of Jem's Subaru, piled high with gear.

"Sorry!" Ducky said. "Actually I'm not, but I'll pretend that I am because we're friends."

"Where the hell am I supposed to put my amp?" I asked.

"Why don't you put it in your own car?"

"Because my car is full of luggage," I replied.

Rose stepped forward and wordlessly rearranged the gear enough for me to slide my amp in beside the drums.

"Thanks," I said. "You're a considerate bandmate." I glared at Ducky, who just grinned.

"Okay!" Jem called out. "Reminder of tour rules!"

Ducky rolled her eyes good-naturedly. Jem came and stood in front of us.

"Number one," she said. "No snacks on the band credit card. This is only for gas and lodging."

"I'm probably gonna break that rule," I said. "But if I do, I'll pay you back."

"Please try to just keep the rule," Jem replied. "Number two, no drinking until after our set is done."

"Aye aye, captain," Ducky said.

"Number three, be smart."

Ducky raised her hand.

"Yes, Ducky," Jem said.

"Does being smart still include having sex with audience members?" Ducky asked.

"If you want," Jem sighed.

Ducky did an exaggerated fist pump.

"Here come the boys," Rose said.

I looked up to see a van pulling up in front of our run-down Victorian-mansion-turned-apartment. Spray-painted on the side of the van were the words "The Boy Scouts of Atlantis."

Which included Simon.

Simon and I hadn't spoken since that night at the venue when he used my guitar pick. There was some friendly banter after the show, but then they left to play the East coast, for three months. I had spent that time working here and there and playing shows and occasionally wondering what bands Simon liked. And he and his band were back to join us on our West coast tour, which was going to be an entire month, and then they were leaving again to play another gig in like, Colorado or some shit.

And even though we'd only spoken a few times, I kept having daydreams about Simon and I on this tour together. Not that I was even sure he would be interested in me. He was flirty at that show but sometimes rock band guys are just like that. Some of them have got that charismatic thing onstage that makes everyone swoon but in real life, so many of them are actually really boring, or else actually really misogynistic. I didn't know if Simon's onstage charisma was who he really was or not.

I guess I was going to find out. I tried not to stare at Simon sitting in the driver's seat.

Damn, he was just as good-looking as I remembered. His curly brown hair was gathered into a bun, and he was wearing a green t-shirt that I could just imagine was bringing out his eyes.

The van slowed to a stop behind my Honda, and the door slid open. "Ready to hit the open road?" a cheerful voice asked.

Aaron was the bassist for the Boy Scouts of Atlantis, and he looked like a blonde Clark Kent. All-American, Brawny paper towel man, Captain America type.

"Ready!" Ducky replied, grinning.

"Well, pile that extra gear on in here!" he gestured.

Jem was already walking toward the van with a handful of mic stands.

"Hurry up," Felix called out from the passenger seat.

Rose had known Felix for years, but he didn't really come over much, so my only impression of him so far was that of a grumpy black cat, and based on his current tone of voice, I thought I was probably right. He was even dressed in black, head to toe, and his messy black hair kept falling into his eyes. Which were also lined in black. Straight up emo kid. (And also a helluva keyboardist.)

Another guy climbed out of the van, slipping a leather notebook into his pocket.

"Wendy, right?" I asked.

He held out his hand. "Wendover, but yeah, everyone calls me Wendy." He gave me the tenderest handshake, which was completely surprising, because he was an absolute animal on the drums. Offstage, he looked like he slipped into this reality from another timeline. Like, he could wear suspenders and a newsboy cap and it would look completely normal on him. He had the kind of Victorian mystery-boy cheekbones that you would find in a being from another realm.

"Nice to meet you," I said, smiling.

The next few minutes were good-natured chaos, while we tried to fit all of our extra gear into the boys' van, alongside all of their gear. This task mostly consisted of Felix grumbling, and Simon and Wendy smiling at Felix's grumbling, and Aaron cheerfully getting in everyone's way. Finally, we were ready.

"Okay!" Jem called out. "Gather round!" We all stood near the van's open door. "Okay, gang," she said. "It's a one-hour drive to Petaluma, not including traffic, and sound check is at 4, so let's get to the motel by 2 pm."

"HUA," Aaron replied, saluting Jem with a grin.

"Text if something comes up," Jem replied.

The boys all climbed into their van while Rose and Jem made their way to Jem's Subaru. Ducky followed me to my Honda.

Once we were on the road, I turned to Ducky and grinned. "West Coast tour!" I shouted.

"West Coast tour!" she shouted back. Then she picked up the walkie-talkie from the dashboard and yelled the same thing into it.

Jem's voice came crackling back. "Yes, West Coast Tour. You don't need to yell. Over."

"Love you, Jem. Over," Ducky said.

"Love you back. Over."

I could hear Jem's smile through the walkie-talkie. Ducky put on a road trip playlist and we made our way toward the freeway.

"It's weird to think of Felix and Rose being friends in high school," I said.

"I was going to say the same thing!" Ducky replied. "He's so…edgy anarchy boy, and Rose is like, the most precious, sweet, quiet darling in the world."

"Apparently, they did drama together. Like, tech stuff."

"I guess I can see that." Ducky stared out the window for a while, nodding along to the Black Keys. "What do you think of the rest of the boys?"

I shrugged, trying to act as nonchalant as possible. "They seem nice," I said. "Aaron is a golden retriever boy and that's kind of the best."

"And Wendy?"

"Okay, is it just me, or is he like, a demon on the drums and a weird Victorian changeling boy in real life?"

"He is a weird Victorian changeling boy!" Ducky laughed. "What about Simon?"

I paused, trying to figure out how to answer. "He's a good frontman for a rock band." I glanced over to see Ducky smirking at me. "What?"

"Nothing," Ducky replied. When I didn't answer, she added, "He just seems like the kind of guy who could easily distract you from your goals."

"I won't get distracted!" I retorted. I didn't correct her on the kind of guy Simon was, though.

"Eyes on the prize, my friend," she said. "Pacific Northwest music festivals. Bumbershoot. Sasquatch. Timber."

"It's going to be so sick when we get accepted to play Sasquatch," I replied. "All I want is to play Sasquatch."

"Same."

"Actually, all I want is to just keep playing music until it's truly and actually my job," I added. "No more Task-

Rabbit, no more temp agencies, no more substitute teaching. Just music. We're so close."

At this point, we actually managed to make an okay amount of money with the band. Rose was the only one of us who had anything close to a regular job, working part-time at a plant nursery in downtown Alameda. Jem taught private guitar lessons, and the rest of us paid the bills by working odd jobs.

"We're on our way," Ducky said.

I couldn't help smiling. "It really feels that way," I said.

THERE IS something magical about a music venue. I'd never played a stadium, and I didn't know if I ever would. But I think I would miss small stages in bars and garages and warehouses. Petaluma's venue had a set of risers for the musicians, all covered in gray industrial carpeting, decades of gaff tape residue pressed into the fibers. I could smell cigarette smoke wafting in from the back door. A couple of the stage lights were so old that I could smell the layer of dust on them burning. It was perfect.

The Boy Scouts of Atlantis were as good onstage as I remembered. Simon was up there, all hair and hands and lyrics, and both my ears and my libido had strong feelings about all of it. He communicated more with his band mates than I had noticed back in April. And not just between songs. He'd turn to each of the guys in turn, jamming with them, trading solos, laughing. They all genuinely looked like they were having *fun*. They were still focused, but they were having a blast.

It made playing after them even more fun. I don't think I ever forgot that playing music was fun, but there were definitely shows when things were off, or the crowd was quiet or really small, or we were all exhausted. Petaluma was one of those magical nights when everything was just...*fun*.

I tried new things on a few solos, and Jem was on fire, and Rose and Ducky were so steady behind me. We finished our set sweaty and happy, and I couldn't imagine a better start to the tour.

CHAPTER 2

The Oregon Rule

JULY 6: PETALUMA, CALIFORNIA TO FORT BRAGG, CALIFORNIA

SIMON

It was a good thing I liked my bandmates, because this van was not big enough for the four of us *and* a bunch of gear. And we just spent all night in a shitty motel together. While we're on the road, we rotate who drives so that everyone can get a break. I would take a nap right now if Felix wasn't driving twenty miles over the speed limit. At least Wendy and Aaron let me have shotgun again. I looked out of the window for a while before Felix spoke.

"Thoughts on our first show?"

"Good as hell," I replied. "Queen Anne is really good."

Felix nodded. "They're a good match for our sound. They've got a Bree Sharp, No Doubt, Sleater-Kinney thing going on."

I thought back to watching their set, each of the women just absolutely owning that stage. Jem was an icon, commanding the crowd and singing her brains out. Rose was as steady on bass as Ducky was chaotic on the drums. (Chaotic in attitude, not in rhythm.) Although, if I'm being honest with myself, my gaze kept being drawn to Marlowe. Her long brown hair, braided into a crown on the top of her head. Her deep blue eyes. Her dark lipstick making every movement of her mouth mesmerizing.

The drive to Fort Bragg was two and a half hours, so I had already had plenty of time to think about it.

When we pulled into the Motel 6 parking lot, Ducky was yelling something as she exited the Honda.

"What?" Wendy asked, sliding the door of the van open. I stepped out into the parking lot and stretched.

"We've decided you guys need a walkie talkie too!" Ducky repeated. "So we're going to the store!"

"But first, we should get dinner, because I'm starving." That statement came from Marlowe, who was climbing out of the driver's seat of the Honda.

"There's a good pizza place a few blocks from here," Felix said.

"What's this about a walkie-talkie?" I asked.

Ducky held one up. "We always bring these on tour to communicate when we're in separate cars and you guys should have one, too."

Felix frowned. "What's wrong with cell phones?" he asked.

Ducky rolled her eyes. "This is more fun, dumbass. And safer for when you're driving."

Aaron stumbled out of the van, rubbing his eyes. "Are we there?" he asked. "I'm starving."

"We're gonna get pizza," I said. "But you're paying."

Aaron looked at me blankly. "I am?"

I grinned at him. "No, but you really believed me for a second."

He shook his head, looking wide-eyed.

An orange Subaru pulled into the parking lot, and Rose and Jem stepped out. "Okay!" Jem called out. "What's the plan?"

Marlowe answered. "Pizza, store for an extra walkie talkie, then whatever anyone wants."

"Copy that," Jem said. She replaced her cap on her mullet, red hair spilling out onto one shoulder and blonde on the other.

I hid a smile. I was learning that while Jem was wild and free onstage, she was militantly organized offstage. Which, honestly, was helpful. Every band should have at least one member who's organized. This whole tour existed because of Jem and Felix. Between their spreadsheets and itineraries, they ran a tight ship.

The pizza place Felix recommended was tiny and dimly lit—a little mom and pop place where every single surface was covered in a thin film of grease.

It was perfect.

The eight of us squeezed into one long booth, and just by chance, I ended up next to Marlowe. Her thigh pressed along mine, and when she turned to say something to Rose on her other side, I caught a whiff of her hair.

She smelled amazing. Floral and sweet.

I was still getting to know everyone. I repeated their names to myself as I glanced around the table. There was Rose, small and quiet, with her soft brown eyes and wavy brown pixie cut hair. Jem, with her piercing green eyes that were honestly a little intimidating, but her full sleeve tattoos probably intensified the badass factor. Ducky was loud and chaotic and kind, with bright purple hair that went down to her shoulders, and piercings all up and down her ears, as well as one in her nose.

She turned to Felix sitting on the other side of me.

"So," she said. "Are we the best band you've ever toured with?"

"The tour just started," Felix replied.

"But still!" Ducky insisted.

"Sound?" Felix said. "Great. Vibes? Yet to be determined."

Ducky grinned.

"As long as there are no major disasters while on this tour, I'm happy," Jem said.

"We haven't really ever had any major disasters on tour," Wendy said thoughtfully. He looked at me for confirmation.

I thought for a moment. "There was one time when we were on tour with this other band and Aaron almost got into a fistfight because some guy in the other band thought he was flirting with their bassist."

"Oh, yeah!" Aaron said. "I forgot about that!"

"They should have just trusted The Oregon Rule," Felix said, taking a sip of his drink.

"What's 'The Oregon Rule'?" Jem asked, frowning.

Felix turned to her. "The Oregon Rule is that no one ever hooks up with any member of a band we're playing shows with. Or on tour with."

I glanced at Marlowe. I couldn't help it. Our eyes caught for one brief second before she looked down at the table, playing with a straw wrapper.

It's not like I was thinking Marlowe and I would hook up on this tour. I mean, maybe I was, I don't know. I didn't even know if she was single, or interested. All I knew was that she smelled good and she was a helluva guitar player and that I couldn't stop staring at her ruby red lips when she was onstage. Which I guess meant I was interested.

But on this tour, she was strictly off limits, and after this tour, the Boy Scouts were leaving for two weeks.

"That's not going to be a problem, is it?" Felix asked. He made it sound like a threat.

"The Oregon Rule?" Jem asked. "Definitely not a problem. That's actually genius." Jem turned to the rest of the members of Queen Anne. "We should have an Oregon Rule."

Rose, Ducky, and Marlowe all just looked at her. She turned back to Felix. "What are the parameters?"

"No kissing, no sex of any kind, no romantic shit. If two weeks has passed since playing with another band, the Oregon Rule no longer applies. And audience members are fine."

"Thank god audience members are fine," Ducky said.

"And it's never been a problem for you guys?" Jem asked.

"Nope," Felix said.

"True," Aaron replied.

"Never been a problem," Wendy said.

"What about him?" Ducky asked, pointing at me.

"Me?" I asked, raising my eyebrows. I could have sworn I felt Marlowe's muscles tense next to me.

"He won't break any rules," Aaron answered on my behalf. He leaned forward and whispered, "Simon might give off bad boy rocker vibes, but I've known this guy since kindergarten, and he's never broken a rule in his life."

"Really?" Marlowe asked.

I turned to see her looking up at me. Good god, those blue eyes. I felt suddenly self-conscious. "Kind of?" I said.

"Not kind of," Wendy said. "He's never gone over the speed limit. He won't watch bootlegs of shows. The man won't even jay-walk."

Marlowe's eyes roamed over my face. "That…surprises me," she said.

I shrugged. "I just…try to be respectful? I guess."

"Feel free to make fun of him for it," Wendy said. "We always do."

Marlowe leaned to playfully push at my shoulder with hers. "As long as making fun of him doesn't break a rule," she said.

"Marlowe is a rule-BREAKER," Jem said. "Most of the time."

Marlowe took a sip of her Pepsi and shrugged. "What can I say? I hate authority."

~

BACK AT THE motel (after a stop at Walmart for an extra walkie talkie), the girls all said good night and closed the door to their room. Wendy, Felix, Aaron and I all hauled our bags into the room next door.

The greatest idea we have ever had was to bring an X-box on tour. Yes, it adds a little more gear, but it's so worth it. Aaron and I always fucking dominated on every part of Hoth in Star Wars Battlefront, and Felix always got pissed and Wendy always just laughed at him, and it was great.

I had a hard time concentrating tonight, though.

I honestly didn't know what I thought would happen between Marlowe and I on this tour. I knew about The Oregon Rule. I believed in The Oregon Rule. Even if something were to happen, the logistics didn't even make sense—like, where would we even go to hook up? Would we kick everyone out of one of the motel rooms and put a sock on the door? Find a corner of a venue and make out in the dark?

I swallowed hard, because actually that sounded awesome.

As soon as I knew it wasn't a possibility, I couldn't stop thinking about it.

In detail.

After Felix and Wendy beat us on one of the Hoth levels for the third time in a row (and after Aaron grumbled at me for it), I switched off my controller. "I'm gonna go to bed," I said.

Fingers crossed my dreams were G-rated. (Or not.)

CHAPTER 3

The Cherry Stem Thing

JULY 7: FORT BRAGG, CALIFORNIA

MARLOWE

I know I'm probably damaging my hearing, like permanently, but I love a loud rock show. I love when you can feel the bass in the cartilage of your nose. When the music blocks out every other thought and feeling and you're just swimming in an ocean of sound.

And the Boy Scouts of Atlantis were playing *loud*. I stood with my other bandmates close to the stage, all four of us dancing and jumping around to the music. I was trying really hard not to be too obvious, but I couldn't take my eyes off of Simon for most of their six-song set. My ridiculous libido aside, it was an objectively good set.

By the time we got onstage, I was especially grateful for that objectively good set, since it had gotten the crowd all hyped. Fort Bragg might be small, but the folks in this venue were hella into the music. We weren't well-known enough that anyone would sing along to any of our songs outside of the Bay Area. But when we covered "Fell In Love With A Girl," the entire room scream-sang along

21

with us, and it was magic. When we finished, I was sweaty and so so so happy.

And then the headliner band was killer. They had this early-2000s, Strokes-y kind of sound, but then they threw in some good old-fashioned metal stuff, and no one could help moving to it. I was standing in front of the stage again, tossing my hair around to the music, when I felt a hand on my upper arm.

I looked up to see Simon standing nearby. He smiled and held out a beer. Which was so sweet that I thought about taking it. But the truth was that I hated beer so much. And I made a decision years ago to never be something other than myself, especially for men.

"*Thanks, but I don't like beer!*" I shouted at him.

"*What?*"

I leaned in closer, and Simon bent down, turning his head so I could speak into his ear. My chest did a little zing at the proximity. "*I said thanks but I don't like beer!*"

Simon straightened and looked down at me. Then he set the beer down on a nearby table. He touched my arm again and leaned down.

Good god, why did he have to smell so good? Something sharp and citrus-y…

And then his lips brushed my ear. "*What do you like?*" he asked.

I tried not to let my knees buckle. Oh, the answers I could give to that question.

I placed a hand on his bicep (oh damn) and stood on my tiptoes. "*Wanna grab me a Shirley Temple?*"

Simon grinned, then disappeared toward the bar. In a few minutes, he returned, carrying two Shirley Temples. He handed me one and clinked his against it.

I smiled, plucked the maraschino cherry from my drink and bit it off its stem.

"*Can you do the thing?*" he leaned down and asked. Another brush of his lips against my ear. "*The cherry stem thing?*"

I gave him a look. "*No one has asked me that since the ninth grade.*"

"*But you know what I'm talking about.*"

I smiled at him and placed the cherry stem in my mouth. A few seconds of manipulation, and I pulled it out of my mouth again, a tidy knot in its center.

Simon looked at it and then grinned at me. "*Nice!*" he said.

I wanted to be close to him again. To feel his heat under my hands and lips. I grabbed his arm and stood on my tiptoes to shout into his ear.

"*Hey, why did the cherry start a band?*" I asked.

"*Why?*"

"*He wanted to JAM.*"

Simon grinned at me again, then reached up to give me a high five.

IT WAS after midnight by the time the last band finished. But after we'd loaded up all our gear, Aaron turned to us in the parking lot. "I'm still all hyped from the show," he said. "Do you guys wanna come over?"

"Sure," I said.

"I'm going to bed," Jem replied.

"I'm not going to bed," Ducky added. "But I will not be coming over."

I looked up to see her smiling at a guy in the bar doorway behind us.

"Be smart," I told her.

"Location services on, condoms in my bag, I'll get an

Uber, call me if I'm not home in three hours. Bring my gear inside for me?"

"You got it," I said. She strode toward the man in the doorway.

I turned to Rose. "You wanna hang with the boys?"

"Okay," she replied.

I turned to Aaron. "What room number are you?"

"106," he said. "We'll leave the door cracked, just come on in."

If I was trying to get into Simon's pants, I would have gone to our own room first, and changed clothes, and fixed my hair, and touched up my makeup, and made sure I smelled okay.

But I was following The Oregon Rule, so I didn't do any of those things.

Or, I didn't do most of them. I just dropped my gear off in the room (and Ducky's) and put on some more deodorant. And kind of fixed my hair.

When Rose and I pushed open the door to room 106, Felix and Wendy were playing on an Xbox, and Aaron and Simon were devouring Taco Bell at a small table.

"Did you guys bring that?" I asked, gesturing to the Xbox.

"It's the best idea we've ever had," Simon answered. I looked at the table.

"The worst idea you've ever had was not asking us if we wanted Taco Bell," I said.

"Good thing we got like, six extra tacos," Aaron replied, pushing a brown paper bag toward me and grinning.

"Hell yes," I said, and sat down next to them. "Rose, do you want any?"

"I'm good," she said. She settled onto the other bed to watch Felix and Wendy play.

I took a bite of one of the tacos, closed my eyes, and stifled a moan. "Why does food always taste so good after a good show?"

When I opened my eyes, it was to find Simon staring at me, and Aaron staring at Simon.

"What?" I asked.

Simon looked away and took another bite of his own food. "It's all the adrenaline," he said.

"Hey, is Ducky okay?" Aaron asked.

"Why?"

"We just left her with that guy at the bar."

I shrugged. "That's Ducky."

When Simon stared at me, I added, "She's following the Oregon Rule. All of you? Off limits. Random guys in bars? Fine."

"But is it safe?" Aaron asked. I looked over at him to see his forehead creased with worry.

I softened. "She'll be fine. She's got rules in place."

"Huge fan of rules," Simon said.

"We know!" Wendy yelled.

"Does she do this a lot?" Simon asked.

"Hook up with people at shows?" I replied. "All the time."

Simon took another bite of his crunchwrap. "Anything serious, ever?"

I shook my head. "Not that I know of. It's just casual with her."

I felt a question hover in my mind—I wanted to know if Simon was the kind of guy who hooked up with people at shows. The answer didn't even matter, but still. I wanted to know. I tried to sound as nonchalant as I could.

"What about you?" I asked. "Ever do one-night stands with your groupies?"

Simon's mouth was full of food, so he took a moment

to answer. "I don't really…date casually," he finally said. "I'm a little bit of an all-or-nothing guy."

I paused. "And is it all or nothing right now?"

"Nothing. There's uh…there's someone I'm interested in, back in the Bay Area. It's hard with all the traveling, but…we'll see."

There was another pause, the sounds of some Star Wars game in the background.

"How about you?" Simon asked.

"Oh," I said. And then, for some dumb reason, I panicked. "I'm kind of in the same situation. Talking with someone, but not serious."

This was not true. At all. And the lie didn't even make sense, because really, I wanted Simon to know I was single, but I didn't know why because the Oregon Rule made it irrelevant anyway.

"Cool," Simon said.

CHAPTER 4

The Trees Here Are Too Fucking Big

JULY 10: REDWOODS NATIONAL PARK,
CALIFORNIA

SIMON

I'd been thinking about what I told Marlowe for three days. About being interested in someone back in the Bay Area. I was thinking about it as I sat behind the wheel of the van, driving to the redwoods. Because it was a total and complete lie. I didn't even know why I said it. Some weird part of me wanted her to think that I was…I dunno, a hot commodity? I felt weirdly embarrassed about how attractive I found her and wanted to play it cool. Which meant lying through my teeth, apparently.

I thought about my lie the whole time we played in Gerberville last night, watching Marlowe up on the stage, all red lipstick and blue eyes and guitar solos. And that girl could *solo*. She would do this thing where she would stare down at the frets and bite her lip, and every now and then, she would strum it all huge and theatrical. Was it weird that I suddenly wanted to be a guitar? Specifically *her* guitar.

We'd only played three shows with them so far, but I

was starting to learn some of their songs. Last night, I sang along to part of "Scissorhood" and when Marlowe caught my eye, she grinned at me.

"Holy shit!" Aaron suddenly exclaimed from the front seat, startling me out of my thoughts.

"What?" I asked.

"These trees are fucking huge!"

I followed his gaze out the window and…

Holy shit.

The trees *were* huge. I'd seen pictures before, but this was otherworldly. Hell, I'd even seen redwoods before, but not like these. These giants towered over us, their trunks four times bigger than our van. They seemed to reach so high up that I couldn't even see the tops of them. I'd been so busy thinking about Marlowe that I hadn't noticed us entering the National Park.

Aaron grabbed the walkie talkie from the center console and spoke into it. "Are you guys seeing this?"

Marlowe's voice crackled in answer. "These trees are insane! Over!"

Aaron turned and yelled over his shoulder. "Felix! Wendy! You gotta see these trees!"

"What the shit are you talking about?" Felix grumbled. I glanced in the rearview mirror to see him rubbing his eyes—he'd clearly been asleep. But then he looked out the window and whispered, "Whoa." Wendy was already staring out the window.

We drove in awed silence until we got to the campground where we were staying. Felix had complained about camping, but Jem pointed out that sleeping in a giant yurt with electricity and heat was barely camping.

I agreed with her, and I was a fan of the "camping" idea. We had a couple of days before our next gig in

Eureka, and I couldn't think of a better way to spend it than in the redwoods.

Even if it meant sleeping in the same room as Marlowe.

Which was totally fine. All eight of us were going to be sharing the yurt, which sounded fun, even though the thought of Marlowe in pajamas was distracting no matter what version of pajamas my imagination put her in.

We pulled up to the yurt at dusk, and after a dinner of sandwiches and chips, Wendy built a fire. (I swear I didn't know who Wendy was sometimes. He seemed like such a bookish man, but he started that fire without matches? Like an *actual* Boy Scout?). As the sun set, I pulled my guitar out of its case and sat in a chair, noodling around. I'd been digging on 7th chords lately. I kind of hit on a rhythm, so I played through the progression a few times.

"The trees here are too fucking big," Aaron sang. Or attempted to sing.

I grinned at him. Aaron is a famously bad singer. Like, he can barely sing through the bass line of a song—at practice, he always has to just demonstrate what he's talking about on his bass, because none of us know what he's referencing if he tries to sing it.

I played through the chord progression again, and sang along with Aaron. "The trees here are too fucking big!"

By the time we sang it a third time, almost everyone else had joined in.

"I thought I knew what trees were," Wendy sang. "But I did not know shit…"

"These trees are bigger than my ex's ego," Ducky added.

Marlowe finished the phrase. "And that man was not the tits!"

"Chorus!" I yelled. "The trees here are too fucking big!"

Half an hour later, Wendy had transcribed all of our lyrics, and Marlowe had grabbed her guitar and joined in, and we had an actual (stupid but catchy) song about the redwoods. Jem and Felix were arguing about some part of the song when Marlowe sat down in the chair next to me.

"Hey, let me know what we owe you for the walkie talkie," I said.

Marlowe looked at me. "Oh," she said. "I stole it."

My eyes widened. "You…*stole* it?"

She shrugged. "That giant-ass big box store doesn't need my money, and fuck billionaires."

My ethics were feeling kind of scrambled. Because stealing was wrong, and I knew it was wrong, but it somehow didn't seem as bad when Marlowe put it that way? Was it just because she was hot that I was willing to overlook it?

"Okay," I said, not knowing what else to say.

"Are you really a big rule-follower?" Marlowe asked.

I turned to her, the firelight making her blue eyes look deep and full. I sighed. "I really am," I answered. "I really really want to be a rebel. I'm just…not."

"That's kind of…"

"Dumb?" I finished.

Marlowe smiled. "Not necessarily."

"'Not necessarily'?"

"I mean," Marlowe continued, "In some people it can be dumb." She glanced over her shoulder and lowered her voice. "Jem can get a little controlling about it sometimes. But somehow it doesn't seem dumb when you do it."

What she said was so innocuous, but it was making me feel…unzipped? Like she had pulled on something and now my insides were on display.

"Thanks. I think."

She studied me. "Why?"

"Because I think you just paid me a compliment?" I said.

"No, I mean why do you follow the rules?"

I turned my focus to the fire. "I think…I think because most of them are there for a reason. To protect people, or keep things safe. I want to respect that." I turned to look at Marlowe again.

"What if some of the rules are there to just protect the wealthy elite and the oppressive establishment?" she asked.

I raised my eyebrows. "Do some of the rules do that?"

Marlowe raised her eyebrows back. "Uh, *yeah*."

"Like what rules?"

"Um, drug laws?" she said. "Parking tickets and towing policies? Any law about 'loitering.' All the random-ass fines people have to pay to navigate the legal system?"

"Drugs harm people," I countered.

But Marlowe shook her head. "But the law doesn't protect people equally. For years, the sentence for crack cocaine was way higher than for powder, even though powder is more expensive. If you're rich, you can afford to pay fines, and if you're not, you go to jail. Which also means lost wages and a record and all kind of other shit. Laws are literally just fines for rich people."

"What about the laws that really do help everyone? Like…" I searched my thoughts. "Littering laws?"

Marlowe smiled. "I'm just saying," she said. "Some rules are worth breaking." I felt her gaze on my face…I didn't just see it, I *felt* it—as if her look was actually touching me, like I could feel her fingers running over my features. I looked back at her, her eyes softly blazing. And I couldn't help it, my gaze slipped down to her lips, full and soft.

The timing was very inconvenient, and we'd only known each other a few days, but Jesus Christ, I wanted to kiss her. Bad.

I was very very aware of the weight of what she had just said…that some rules were worth breaking. Did that include the Oregon Rule? Because I really wanted to break the Oregon Rule. I wanted to cup Marlowe's jaw and tangle my hands into her hair and—

"Simon!" Aaron called out.

It broke me out of my reverie. "Huh?" I asked, turning.

"What were the chords to the tree song you were just doing?" Aaron had pulled his bass out of the van and was sitting with it in his lap.

I wrapped my hand around the neck of my guitar and played through them again. "D seven, D major seven, D major."

"Kiss Me," Marlowe said.

My brain shorted out.

"Huh?"

"The chords," Marlowe. "Kiss Me. Sixpence None the Richer. D seven, D major seven, D major."

Oh.

Marlowe strummed the chords on her own guitar and started singing. "Kiss me, out of the bearded barley. Nightly, beside the green green grass." Her voice was low and sultry, a slight smile playing over her lips.

From across the campfire, Ducky joined in. "Swing, swing, swing the spinning step."

Aaron added his own warbly voice. "You wear those shoes and I will wear that dress!"

And then it was all of us. I watched Marlowe's fingers, picking up on the rest of the chords. By the time we got to the second chorus, I did a little solo over the first stanza, and then she did one over the second.

I grinned at her. She grinned back.

CHAPTER 5

Compliments & Sweatshirts

JULY 10: REDWOODS NATIONAL PARK, CALIFORNIA

MARLOWE

This was why I loved music. And going on tour with awesome people. So that we could make up dumb songs about trees and then jam on Sixpence None The Richer.

After we played through the song's verses in no actual order, Aaron tilted his head back and exclaimed "Ugggghhhh, I love D chords!"

"You love deez NUTS," Simon replied. "Speaking of which, I'm going to the bathroom." He stood.

"Take a picture for your Instagram account!" Ducky called out.

I blinked at her. Because I could not make sense of what she had just said.

"What Instagram account?" I asked, frowning.

"You don't know about Simon's Instagram account?" Ducky asked.

"How do *you* know about Simon's Instagram account?"

I countered. "And what does it have to do with… his…nuts?"

"I'm a cultured bitch," Ducky replied. "And it doesn't have anything to do with Simon's nuts. At least not directly." She was pulling out her phone. I glanced over at Simon, who was very intentionally not looking at any of us while he leaned his guitar in his camp chair.

"It's not a big thing," he said. "I just like doing it."

Ducky handed me her phone, open to an Instagram account called "Meet Me In the Bathroom." I set my guitar back into its case and grabbed the phone.

"Holy shit, you have like, 90,000 followers," I said. I was about to say something more, but then I started scrolling through the photos and forgot what I was going to say.

The feed was filled with hundreds of photos of venue bathrooms. Which sounded weird, but it was actually… beautiful? The photos emphasized the art on the walls, or the messages scribbled in sharpie, or the stickers on the mirrors. There were close-ups of graffiti and peeling layers of wallpaper. There was a zoomed in shot of what was almost definitely cocaine powder on a toilet paper dispenser. A blurry shot of someone's mouth, a joint in their pursed lips.

Somehow Simon managed to capture all of the punk beauty and messy humanity of rock venues on this Instagram account and I was suddenly obsessed.

"Simon," I said. "These are…these are amazing." But when I looked up, he wasn't there. He must have still been in the bathroom. "Oh," I said. "Never mind, I guess he doesn't get the compliment."

"Probably for the best," Wendy said. "If there's one thing Simon hates more than breaking rules, it's getting compliments."

"That sounds like a challenge," Ducky grinned.

"Maybe the guy just needs a little exposure therapy," Jem added.

"What do I need?" Simon asked, striding back into the firelight.

"You're a great photographer!" Wendy said.

Simon frowned at him and kept making his way to his chair next to mine. I smiled and picked up the mug of hot chocolate I'd left on the ground beside us. It may have been summer, but nights got chilly in the redwoods.

"The internal rhyme scheme of 'Single Serving Friends' is the shit," Felix added.

Rose smiled up at Simon from her place next to Felix. "I like your shoes."

Simon picked up his guitar, but stayed standing. Which, I'm not gonna lie, put him at an…advantageous level for my eyes. The pants he was wearing were doing wonders for his ass, and when he turned to the side…

Okay, let's not compliment him on that.

How about something adjacent?

"The way you move your hips when you sing could destroy nations!" I said, looking up at him.

His eyes met mine, a flash of heat and surprise in his gaze. A zing went through me, and I swallowed, not looking away.

Ducky's voice cut through. "Your Instagram rips!"

Simon broke my gaze and looked around in alarm. "What is happening right now?"

"We're complimenting you, my man," Aaron said, with all the innocence and charm of a Norman Rockwell painting.

Simon sat down and put his guitar in front of his face. "Well, I don't like it."

"But we like *you*," Ducky said.

Simon turned to look at me from where he was ducking his head behind his guitar, and fuck, if he didn't look adorable.

I grinned at him and raised my mug of hot chocolate in his direction.

"Okay, well now I need to go put my guitar away because I don't want to deal with you people being nice to me," Simon said. He stood, but stumbled slightly, knocking into my hot chocolate. A wave of liquid sloshed over the sleeve of my jacket.

"Shit!" Simon said. "Oh no! I'm sorry!"

Ducky laughed. "You're really good at spilling things!"

"Don't be mean," Rose admonished.

"I'm continuing the compliment game," Ducky said.

I pulled off my jacket and looked up at Simon, who was looking at me with genuine distress. "Let me get you another jacket," he pleaded.

"I…don't have another one," I replied. I was about to say that I could go get a blanket from inside the yurt, but then Simon was pulling his sweatshirt over his head. His shirt rode up underneath it before he tugged it back down, and the sight of his bare stomach and chest was distracting enough that I legitimately forgot what I was about to say.

"Here," he said.

"I'm not taking your sweatshirt," I told him.

"But it's my fault your jacket is all wet."

I looked at him. And thought that I really needed to get laid, not just because Simon's jawline was looking really edible, but because my mind had snagged on his use of the word "wet" like I was some kind of seventeen-year-old horndog.

Simon was still holding his sweatshirt out to me, his eyes looking all imploring, and how was I supposed to resist? It was the least logical solution to the problem—it literally made more sense for me to get a blanket to wrap around myself to keep warm. But he was standing there, all brown curls and pleading hazel eyes and yummy forearms, and I couldn't bring myself to say no.

I reached out and pulled the sweatshirt over my head. The fabric was warm and dry and oh god, it smelled like Simon's delicious citrus-y *boy* smell.

"What are you gonna wear?" I asked.

Simon shrugged. "I have another jacket in the car, but it's not that bad out here." He settled back into his camp chair, pulling his guitar into his lap. His fingers moved over the strings absently, picking out some lovely melody, as he stared into the fire.

It had been fully dark for a while now, and I stole a glance at Simon's profile. The firelight moved over his features, and a small smile softened his lips as he listened to the others talking.

I thought about my question at the beginning of the tour five days ago—wondering if he was just charismatic onstage and boring or misogynistic offstage. Now that we'd done a few shows together and spent more time together, I could see that Simon definitely turned the charisma *up* when he was onstage. But he was charming offstage too. Just in a different way. I thought about him defending laws against littering and smiled to myself.

"Where did you get the idea for your Instagram?" I asked him.

He turned to me, and I felt my breath catch a little. (He was so *hot*.)

"It was actually Wendy's idea," he replied. "I'd been taking pictures of venue bathrooms for years because…I dunno, because there was always cool shit to take pictures of, and Wendy suggested I start an Instagram."

"It's really fucking cool," I told him. And it was hard to

tell in the firelight, but I thought I saw a faint blush creep across his cheeks.

"Thanks," Simon said quietly. He played his guitar for a few more moments. "Are you warm enough?" he asked.

I smiled at him and pulled the hood of his sweatshirt over my head. "Cozy as hell," I replied. "Thanks."

Simon simply nodded, returning my smile, then turned his attention back to the fire.

AT SOME POINT, between the murmured conversations and soft guitar sounds around the campfire, I must have fallen asleep, because I woke to Simon's hand on my arm.

"Hey," his voice said, a soft whisper.

"Hi," I said, blinking. I shifted in my chair, my neck sore from sleeping at an odd angle. Simon was leaning over me, his face close to mine.

"Come to bed," Simon whispered.

It took me a full fifteen seconds of staring at him to understand what he was saying. Because I could not think of anything I wanted to do more than come to Simon's bed. (Or come *in* Simon's bed.) But I was pretty sure that wasn't what he was saying, even though I couldn't quite remember why he wouldn't. I finally got my brain to comprehend that Simon was suggesting that I sleep in my own bed, in the yurt, and not in a chair by a now cold fire pit.

I sat up, looking around. We were the only ones still out. I could see a light on in the yurt, and hear voices laughing.

"How long was I asleep?" I asked. My voice was a little scratchy.

"Not too long," Simon replied. "Maybe half an hour."

He straightened and held his hand out to help me up. I took it, a small zing going through me as I stood.

But he dropped my hand as soon as I was steady on my feet. I swallowed.

"Did someone bring my guitar inside?" I asked. Simon nodded.

I started to pull his sweatshirt off. "Here," I said.

But Simon grabbed the hem with both hands and held it, his arms straightening to keep the sweatshirt on my body. He stood close, his knuckles inches away from my hipbones.

"Keep it," he whispered.

Then he turned around and walked into the yurt. I followed on shaking legs.

CHAPTER 6

Weird Walks and Tattoo Talks

JULY 11: REDWOODS NATIONAL PARK, CALIFORNIA TO EUREKA, OREGON

SIMON

Sleeping in the same room as Marlowe last night was torture. She was way on the other side of the yurt, but it was a small yurt. I kept thinking about her, wearing my sweatshirt, warm and soft in her bed. If the yurt had come equipped with a cold shower, I would have gotten into it. I finally put my ear buds in and fell asleep to a podcast.

In the morning, Marlowe held my sweatshirt out and smiled at me, and it made my bones feel funny and I wanted to give my sweatshirt to her every night just so she could try to give it back to me every morning. But I kind of wanted her to keep wearing it more.

"You can hold onto it," I said. She shrugged and threw it back on over her head, flashing me a smile.

We spent part of the morning exploring the redwoods, all of us except Felix and Rose, who stayed behind to keep an eye on our gear. The height of those trees was truly mind-blowing. Wendy kept humming the tune of the song we had written about them, and it started out jokingly, but after a while it took on the reverence of a prayer. I don't think he even realized he was doing it.

We didn't have a gig until tomorrow night, so we took our time driving the one hour to Eureka. When we got to the Airbnb that afternoon, almost everyone went to go take a nap. But I was wide awake, despite hardly sleeping last night. Marlowe caught my eye and held my gaze for a moment.

"Wanna go on a weird walk with me?" she asked.

"What's a weird walk?"

"It's where I go on a walk until I find something weird."

I grinned at her. "Have you ever thought of starting an Instagram?"

She returned my grin. "Old Town Eureka is just a few blocks away."

We stepped outside and I fell into stride beside her. I stole a glance at her profile. Her dark hair was up in two buns, and she wore a series of chokers around her neck. One of these days I would develop a cooler sense of style, but today I was wearing my usual daily uniform of pants, band t-shirt, and open button-up.

"So what qualifies as 'weird'?" I asked. "On a weird walk?"

"I'll know it when I see it," Marlowe replied.

"That's not enough of an explanation. I need to know what to be on the look out for."

Marlowe cocked her head in thought. "Abstract art in someone's front yard," she said. "Someone wearing a costume in a place where people don't usually wear costumes. A cardboard cut out of a celebrity in someone's living room window."

"Are all of these things you've seen?"

Marlowe nodded, a small smile playing around her lips.

She was so fucking cool.

"Okay," I said. "My weird-o-meter is…ready."

"Got it calibrated?"

I nodded. As we got closer to Old Town Eureka, the buildings took on a Victorian flair. Even though we came from the San Francisco Bay Area where we saw this kind of architecture all the time, I was still charmed.

I paused at the window of an antique shop, then pointed at the display featuring what looked like an animatronic pig waving a butcher knife.

"Weird?" I asked, turning to Marlowe.

Her eyes widened with delight. "What the hell is this?"

"Terrifying?" I offered.

Marlowe nodded, but she didn't look scared at all. "This is definitely weird," she said. "But not 'weird walk ending' weird."

"Wait, the walk ends when you find something weird?"

Marlowe nodded.

I suddenly didn't want to find anything weird for a while.

But it was fun to look at a new place through this lens. I noticed things I never would have seen otherwise. I paid closer attention to the people walking past, the signs on the buildings. Marlowe was mostly quiet, and I took my cue from her, both of us just looking around us as we walked.

Suddenly, Marlowe stopped in her tracks. She grabbed my hand, and I couldn't help but startle a little at the intimacy of it. I turned to look at her. "What?" I asked. She pointed, and I followed her gaze.

About half a block in front of us was someone dressed as a cigarette—one of those inflatable costumes. I had no idea where you would even find something like that, but the other notable thing was that the cigarette was also dressed for a night on the town. A bright pink feather boa was flung around its body, and peeking out from beneath the bottom of the costume were six-inch high heels.

Marlowe and I exchanged a look, and without even saying a word to each other, I knew we were about to follow this cigarette as long as we could. She was still clutching my hand as we slowly walked forward.

A person in an inflatable cigarette costume was pretty extraordinary, but it was kind of being overshadowed by the sensation of Marlowe's hand in mine. I didn't want to let go. We followed the cigarette for about one block, before it turned and walked into a tattoo shop. Marlowe and I came and stood in front of the large window, trying to look inside without looking too obvious.

"Dude, we should get tattoos," Marlowe said.

"That feels like a really permanent excuse to follow this cigarette person."

"Actually…" Marlowe cocked her head to the side. "We should just…get tattoos."

I frowned at her. "Right now?"

Her eyes flashed over to me, something slightly daring moving over her face. "Yes."

"But…why? What?"

"Because I've thought about getting a tattoo for years and why not right now?"

"But what about me?" I asked.

Marlowe studied me. "Do you have any good reason *not* to get a tattoo today?"

I thought for a moment. And the truth was that I didn't really. I wasn't totally sure how much tattoos cost, but I could probably afford it. I wasn't really afraid of needles, and we didn't have anywhere we needed to be. And it's not like I had a job where tattoos would be a problem.

"I…guess not," I answered.

"So come on, live a little." She nudged me with her shoulder.

"This feels…impulsive," I replied.

"But not dangerous," Marlowe said, shrugging.

"You don't know that," I protested, but even I knew it was a weak argument.

Marlowe folded her arms and looked at me. Her blue eyes were bright with challenge. "Is this breaking a rule?"

"Getting a tattoo? Not really. But—"

Before I could finish my sentence, Marlowe grabbed my hand and dragged us into the tattoo shop. A bell above the door rang and a woman at the desk looked up at us.

"Do you take walk-ins?" Marlowe asked.

"Yeah, the two of you?" the woman asked.

"Yep," Marlowe said. She turned to me. "Unless it's just me?"

Her question hung in the air between us. She was giving me an out if I really wanted it, letting me make the final decision for myself.

But the more I thought about it, the more I couldn't think of any reason *not* to get a tattoo right now. Yes it was impulsive, but maybe I could do with a little push outside of my comfort zone.

"It's the two of us," I said.

The woman at the desk nodded. "Charlie and Antonia are both free. Sign these and they'll come chat with you."

Marlowe and I took the clipboards she handed us and sat down.

"What are you getting?" I asked her.

She gazed up at the ceiling for a moment, thinking. "A guitar tuner," she said decisively. She looked over at me and smiled. "What about you?"

I returned her smile. I had thought of something

music-related, too. "The envelope that guitar strings come in."

"I love that," Marlowe said. She leaned over toward me. "The real question is *where* are you getting your tattoo?" Her eyes slid up and down my body, and my jeans began to feel a little too tight. I shifted in my seat.

"Probably my upper arm," I said. "Like…bicep."

Marlowe's eyes lingered on the spot where I had just gestured, and if she kept looking at my body like that, we were going to have a whole *situation* in my jeans. I swallowed.

"What about you?" I asked.

Which was actually a bad idea to ask. Because now it was my turn to think about Marlowe's body…her lithe arms, her strong muscular thighs, her…

"My *ass*," Marlowe declared.

I blinked at her.

"Just kidding, I'm doing upper arm, too."

And then two different tattoo artists were coming up to us to take our forms and ask what we wanted and we were being led to different chairs and someone was sticking a paper stencil to my arm and then suddenly I was getting a tattoo. There was a split second right before the needle hit my skin when I wondered what the hell I was doing. But Marlowe was right. Getting a tattoo didn't break any rules, and I didn't have any reason not to do it. It hurt less than I thought it would, and after a few minutes, I sank into a kind of unexpected calm.

I glanced over at Marlowe and was startled to find her watching me. Our eyes met and something heated passed between us. I saw her breath hitch slightly as I held her gaze, which I didn't do on purpose, but once her blue eyes locked on mine, I couldn't look away.

Then she grinned at me, and all I could do was grin back.

CHAPTER 7

The Sluttiest Things a Guy Can Do

JULY 13: EUREKA, OREGON

MARLOWE

Maybe it was the break between shows, but our first gig in Eureka last night was objectively not our best. I think all of us sensed a need to step it up tonight, because we crashed into our second gig with guns blazing and it had been killer so far.

The crowd seemed bigger tonight (and maybe drunker), but by the Boy Scouts' second song, they were screaming like it was a K-Pop concert. The rest of Queen Anne and I screamed right along with them.

My eyes kept being drawn to Simon…his forearms… his fingers bending over the strings. The sleeves of his button-up shirt pulled tight over his biceps as he played. I kept trying to tell myself that my interest was purely musical, but the fact that I was clenching my thighs together told a different story.

I gazed up at his face, his jaw tight as he sang into the mic. He had this habit of flipping his hair forward and back again between phrases, moving it out of his way. It was fucking hypnotizing. There was a thin sheen of sweat on his skin, and I had sudden visions of him sweating and tense in other situations, his fingers gripping—

I needed to get ahold of myself.

Just when I'd decided that I needed to calm the hell down, Simon's gaze snagged on mine. And stayed there. One side of his mouth curved up in a smirk as he sang, looking down on me in the crowd.

Jesus Christ.

This was not sustainable. I either had to look away or climb him like a tree and I couldn't do *either*. I was one second away from spontaneous human combustion when he finally shut his eyes tightly to scream into the mic. I screamed, too. Just for a different reason.

When Queen Anne got onstage half an hour later, I did my level best to ignore Simon in the crowd. For most of the show, it wasn't hard—the crowd was genuinely insane by then. I couldn't even see where the Boy Scouts were. Until our last song, "Anarchy Homebody," when all four of them were suddenly right at the edge of the stage, jumping around and yelling. When we got to my guitar solo, I stepped to the front of the stage and balanced one foot on the monitor, giving the music everything I had. I felt a hand curl around my ankle and looked down to see Simon grinning at me, his hand sliding slowly up my calf.

Normally I have kind of a weird relationship with audience members touching me during shows. On the one hand, I like the sense of connection. And sometimes I invite it by leaning into the crowd. Other times, the idea of strangers touching me feels real weird. It's rare that it's invasive, and if it is, it's usually really easy to escape. I've spent years trying to narrow down my philosophy on it and I've concluded that it's a case by case thing.

In this case, I had just discovered that I wanted Simon's

hand on my skin every single second I was onstage, and also I could barely concentrate on my guitar when that was happening.

I bent forward, putting all my weight on the monitor, feeling the heat of Simon's palm on my skin, electrifying every nerve ending. My fingers flew over the frets, and when my solo was over, I stepped back and flashed Simon a grin. He grinned right back.

At the end of the song, the crowd was *feral*—screaming, cheering, pumping their hands in the air. I could hear a few people starting a chant of "one more song!" I glanced over at Jem. We had a go-to encore song, but to be honest, we hadn't played it in a while. But she smiled and nodded. I watched her make eye contact with Ducky on the drums and Rose on bass, and then Ducky counted us off.

Not everyone would recognize a hit by Dr. Teeth and the Electric Mayhem, but Queen Anne could play the shit out of "Can You Picture That?" and it was one of my favorite things. It took me a full year to convince Jem that we should learn it—she kept saying we couldn't do it without a horn section, but between two guitars and us selling it with everything we've got, it rocked every single time.

As soon as the boys realized what we were playing, all four of them burst into cheers, even moody Felix. And even though my fingers were tired, and even though my boots were pinching my feet, and even though I was sweaty and exhausted, I couldn't imagine anything would make me as happy as this.

~

AFTER THE SHOW, all eight of us gathered in the Airbnb kitchen to eat the Chinese takeout we'd ordered.

"Here's to a fucking great second show!" Jem said, raising a can of Sprite into the air.

"Here here!" I echoed.

"It was probably the tattoos," Rose said. "Gave the two of you a rock n' roll edge."

"But we had the tattoos for the first night," I argued, "And that show sucked. I think we were just better tonight."

"What brought on the tattoo thing, anyway?" Wendy asked, picking up an egg roll. Everyone had just sort of taken it in stride when Simon and I had showed up two days ago with fresh ink.

Simon glanced at me. "I'm actually not sure how to explain it…"

I grinned. "We were following someone dressed as a fancy cigarette and then they went into a tattoo shop and then we decided to get tattoos."

"I know even less than I did before," Aaron said.

Felix cocked his head. "You should have gotten it on your thigh," he said to Simon. "Been real slutty about it."

I glanced slyly at my band mates. Because this is a conversation we've had before. And I wasn't totally sure if this was the place to bring that conversation up.

"Ugh, a thigh tattoo is one of the sluttiest things a guy can do," Ducky said.

Never mind, Ducky brought it up. All four boys looked over at her with raised eyebrows.

"I'm serious," Ducky said. "We made a list! Hang on…"

My stomach dropped slightly. I couldn't remember everything that was on that list, but I had a feeling it was about to be incriminating. But that didn't seem like a good enough reason to stop Ducky from sharing it.

She pulled up her notes app on her phone. "Yep, number four: have a thigh tattoo."

Aaron grinned. "What else is on your list of slutty things guys can do?"

"Crop tops," Ducky said. "Three inch inseams."

"Naked flesh," Felix said, nodding.

"Girls like sex!" Ducky exclaimed in reply. "What else? Um, gray sweatpants. Obviously. Also, when a guy wears a button up shirt but he rolls the sleeves up, when he has long hair that he sweeps up into a ponytail, and when he gives you his sweater to wear."

I swallowed and did not look at Simon. I knew that if I looked at him, it would deepen my blush even further. Because even if he wasn't wearing gray sweatpants right now, he was literally wearing a button-up shirt with his sleeves rolled up, and he had swept his hear into a ponytail right before eating, and I definitely still had his sweater in my suitcase downstairs.

I was absolutely right about this list being incriminating.

But apparently I wasn't going to get away with ignoring this moment because Aaron pointed at Simon.

"Slut!" he said.

Simon looked up at us, his head bowed slightly, grinning so adorably I thought I was going to die. He shrugged modestly. "What can I say? Some of us are slutty."

"And some have sluttiness thrust upon them!" Felix added.

"Excellent use of the word 'thrust,'" Rose said.

We bantered about the word "thrust" for a few more minutes before Ducky stood and said she was going to bed. She turned to me. "I'll be up for a little while but if the light is off when you come in, don't wake me up."

I nodded and raised my Sprite in her direction. Ducky

and I always shared a room when we traveled. We'd all been staying in motels and Airbnb's this whole trip so far, although we were staying with some old college friends in Crescent City. After that, we were splitting off from the boys for a few days before meeting up with them again in Corvalis.

And I was not looking forward to the time away from them. We'd only been touring for a week and a half together, but I was already such a fan of these boys.

All of them. Equally. I liked all of them equally.

CHAPTER 8
The Couch is the Bed
JULY 14: CRESCENT CITY, CALIFORNIA

I bent over to lock my pedal board up.

"Hurry up!" Felix called out to me.

"I'm working on it!" I yelled back.

Ducky stuck her head inside the back door of the venue. "No, Felix is right. Hurry up. We can't leave until the two of you are ready and you're taking forever."

I glanced over at Marlowe, who was also packing her gear. Both of us had gotten sucked into conversations with the sound guy, and then suddenly the whole room was empty and our bandmates were yelling at us.

"If you're not out here in five minutes, we're leaving without you," Ducky said.

"You can't leave without me, I'm your ride!" Marlowe replied.

But Ducky just shrugged. "I'll ride with the boys. Simon can go with you."

"What about tomorrow morning?" Marlowe asked.

"Simon has to go with the boys to Lincoln City, and I'm going with you to Brookings."

"No, we're all meeting in Coos Bay first."

Marlowe stood and looked thoughtful. "Oh yeah. That…works, actually," she said.

"We have room for Ducky at our Airbnb," Felix said.

Marlowe looked over at me. "Do you mind staying with me tonight?"

"That's fine with me," I said. I was trying very hard not to think about the rush that went through me at her phrasing. "Where are we staying?"

"With an old friend from college. She and her girl-friend just bought a house."

"Will they miss Ducky?" I asked.

"They don't know Ducky. They moved away before she and I became friends."

I turned back to the doorway, where Ducky and Felix were still standing impatiently. "I'll go with Marlowe," I said. "Will you bring my duffel in here?"

Felix disappeared, grumbling, but I knew he'd be back with my stuff in a minute.

"And I'm grabbing my stuff from your car," Ducky yelled to Marlowe.

I went back to putting away my gear. And I was trying not to read into it, or imagine it into being, but it felt like something hovered in the air between Marlowe and I now, some awareness of the night stretching out in front of us.

Not that anything was going to happen. Obviously. Oregon Rule and all that. It was already past midnight, and we had to leave at 10 the next morning. We were just going to be sleeping in the same building. Like we have before.

"Ready?" Marlowe said. When I looked up at her, my

breath caught for a moment. How were her eyes so *blue*? It made my chest ache.

"Yeah," I said, mentally shaking myself. "Do your friends live far from here?"

"They're only about five minutes away."

God, Marlowe was so hot during that show we just played. I spent most of the drive to her friend's house trying to figure out a way to tell Marlowe how hot she was without like…coming on too strong. Or really coming on at all. I kept trying to phrase it in my mind as a compliment about the music, but every sentence I could come up with made it sound like I wanted to fuck her brains out.

Which, to be fair, I did want to do.

But Oregon Rule. In the end, I didn't say anything.

We pulled up to a small bungalow where two women were smoking on the porch. One of them stood as we got out of the car.

"Marlowe!" she called out.

"Chloe!" Marlowe echoed. The two women hugged, and then Marlowe turned to the other woman on the porch. "You must be Emery. Nice to meet you."

"Nice to meet you. Is this…is this Ducky?"

"Simon," I said, stepping forward to shake her hand.

"What happened to Ducky?" Chloe asked.

"She's staying with some other bandmates," Marlowe answered. "Sorry, is that okay?"

Chloe and Emery exchanged a quick look. "Yeah, that's okay," Chloe said. "We um…if you don't mind sharing a bed?"

My blood caught fire.

"I can sleep on the couch," I said. Probably too quickly.

"Yeah, the um…the couch *is* the bed," Emery said. "It's a sofa bed."

The four of us stood in silence for a moment. It occurred to me that all of us treating this awkwardly was just going to make it more awkward, and that me acting like it was a big deal would just make it seem like there was a deal at all.

"That's fine with me if it's fine with Marlowe," I said.

She turned her gaze to me, and I could have sworn I saw her eyes flash with some kind of quiet heat.

"That's fine," she said. She turned to Emery and Chloe. "Will you help us carry our gear inside?"

The next half hour was stacking amps and guitar cases in the living room (which didn't have a sofa in it, but I figured we'd get to that in a minute), accepting offers of water, declining food, Marlowe and Chloe catching up. Finally, Emery stood from her seat at the kitchen table.

"I'm heading to bed," she said. "Chloe, will you show Marlowe and Simon their room?"

I swallowed.

"Sure," Chloe said. "I'm actually going to head to bed myself. You guys are downstairs. Let me show you."

We followed Chloe down a narrow flight of steps to a small basement with dark paneled wood walls and deep green shag carpet.

"It was renovated in the 70s," Chloe said. She turned to us with a grin. "And Emery and I are both obsessed with it."

"It's incredible," Marlowe said, looking around. Framed embroidery and macrame art decorated the walls, and some aggressively vintage lamps stood on the side tables. And in the middle of the room was a sofa bed, made up with pillows and quilts.

"We've really leaned in to the aesthetic," Chloe replied. "There are extra blankets in the hall cupboard, and you guys have your own bathroom down here. Help yourself to anything in the kitchen or the medicine cabinet. Do you need anything else?"

"We're good," Marlowe said.

"Thanks again," I added.

"Good night!" Chloe said, and then disappeared up the stairs.

Marlowe and I stood side by side, staring at the bed. Two pillows, a blanket. The bed was at least a queen, plenty of room. But still.

"I can sleep on the floor," I offered. Both because I didn't want to make Marlowe uncomfortable, and also because I was actually a little scared of how much I wanted to share this bed with Marlowe.

Marlowe regarded the bed silently for a few moments. Then she glanced around the room. There really wasn't actually much room on the floor. I watched her swallow. "It's fine," she said. She turned to me. "I don't mind sharing the bed if you don't."

I looked at her, and had a sudden memory of the show in Eureka yesterday, of Marlowe's fingers moving like magic over the frets of her guitar, and my hand reaching out to touch her ankle, sliding up her calf. Her grin down at me.

"I don't mind," I said. It came out a little hoarse. "Wanna use the bathroom first?"

"Sure." Marlowe bent to pick up her bag and took a few steps toward the bathroom, then froze.

"What?" I asked.

She turned around. "I um...I don't have pajama pants."

Lord god have mercy.

"What...what did you sleep in when we stayed in the yurt?"

"Ducky's pajama pants. I usually just sleep in a t-shirt and panties."

Lord. God. Have. Mercy.

"Do you…" I paused and tried to get my breathing to return to normal. "Do you want to borrow something?"

She raised her eyebrows at me. "Do you have anything that would fit me?"

"I have um…I might have a pair of boxers."

I couldn't figure out which was more dangerously hot: Marlowe sleeping next to me in just a t-shirt and panties, or Marlowe sleeping next to me in just a t-shirt and panties and *my boxer shorts*.

"That works," she said.

I unzipped my duffel and then tossed her a clean pair of boxers. She caught them and let out a giggle.

"What?" I asked.

"You just threw your underwear at me," she said. Then she gave me a wicked smirk. "Usually this only happens to me when I'm onstage."

I chuckled as she turned and closed the bathroom door behind her. Then I sat on the bed.

Okay, Simon, I thought. *Keep it together.*

I shouldn't break the Oregon Rule. I didn't break rules, ever. And if I was going to start breaking rules, I definitely shouldn't start with this rule.

I could hear Marlowe brushing her teeth, and it was so intimate that it made something in my chest tighten. I really really really liked Marlowe. I could admit that to myself, even if I didn't dare admit it to anyone else.

A few minutes later, the bathroom door opened, and Marlowe walked out, her face clean and bare. My eyes instantly moved down to where my blue boxers were hanging on her hips, the hem reaching the tops of her thighs. Her legs were strong and sturdy, and I could picture them on either side of my ribs while she—

No, look somewhere else.

I moved my gaze upward, but that was the wrong idea, because Marlowe wasn't wearing a bra, and her nipples were pebbling under the fabric of her t-shirt.

When I managed to drag my eyes to her face, she was looking at me intently, her mouth open slightly. Even without her trademark red lipstick, her lips were full and perfect.

I swallowed and tried not to be too obvious about adjusting my jeans.

"Your turn," Marlowe said. I took advantage of her turned back to make my way to the bathroom, my cock straining against my zipper.

CHAPTER 9

Words (and Beds) With Friends

JULY 14: CRESCENT CITY, CALIFORNIA

MARLOWE

I watched Simon close the bathroom door.

I'm wearing his boxers, I thought. I sat down on the bed.

From the bathroom, I heard the metal clinking of Simon's belt buckle being undone, then the whoosh of his belt being pulled off through his belt loops.

I flopped backward onto the bed. This was torture.

In the bathroom, I heard a zipper being pulled down.

I closed my eyes and laid a hand over my crotch. "Calm down," I whispered down to it.

In fact, me and my crotch were going to have to have a serious conversation in the next minute or two, because Simon Burroughs was about to climb into bed next to me, and I was already barely hanging on to the Oregon Rule by a *thread*.

The way he had looked at me before he went to go change…fucking hell. Like he wanted to devour me.

And dear god, I wanted to be devoured.

At least I was pretty sure he wanted to devour me? Not that I had any way of knowing, because of the goddamn Oregon Rule. Like, even if I went for it, Mr. "I always follow all the rules" Simon in there would probably gently push me away whether he was into it or not, because he was so damn upright, and I was coming to adore that about him, even if it was giving me the bluest balls ever.

I heard the shower turn on. I pulled out my phone to scroll TikTok so that I did not think about Simon Burroughs in the shower.

Twenty minutes later, Simon opened the bathroom door, and I glanced up. His hair was wet, and his skin looked delicious.

And god help me. He was wearing gray sweatpants.

Gray. Sweatpants.

Like the goddamn slutty list we had just talked about yesterday. Had I read too many romance novels? Had the internet chronically corrupted me? Or was I just in a permanent state of arousal around Simon, where every-thing he did or said or wore set my blood on fire?

My eyes wandered downward for a split second as he walked toward me. I couldn't help it. His hips narrowed in a way that made me want to grab them, and I could see just enough of a bulge for a rush of heat to spread between my legs. I felt a pinch in my nipples, and pulled the blan-kets more closely over my chest. I managed to drag my eyes back up to his face as he came and stood at the foot of the bed.

"Hey," he said.

"Hey."

A second went by. Then two. Simon looked at the bed in front of him, thinking hard.

"Okay," Simon said. His serious tone made me sit up. His eyes flicked up to me. Were we about to…have a conversation about…what were we about to have a conversation about?

"Yeah?" I said.

"The secret to bed-sharing is separate blankets."

Right.

I was starting to worry that my heart rate would never return to normal. I watched Simon turn around and walk down the hall, then open the cupboard and pull out an extra blanket. He came back and held it up.

"I'll take this one," he said.

I scooted my back farther up the bed so that I was sitting fully up. "I'll take the one I'm currently under," I replied. Simon smiled, and the heat moved from between my legs to my chest, warming me.

"Hop on in, buddy," I grinned.

Simon's smile widened, and he actually physically leaped into the bed. The mattress springs creaked, and I bounced slightly as he landed next to me.

"Oof," I laughed.

"You said 'hop'!" Simon said. He made a production out of arranging his pillow, pulling his blanket up around himself, the bed creaking and moving beneath us until he was fully settled.

"Comfy?" I finally asked, looking down at him from my spot.

He looked up at me with despair in his eyes. "I forgot my phone," he said.

I laughed. "Where is it?"

Simon let out a dramatic sigh and sat up. "No, I'll get it. I can be a big boy."

Why was he so fucking cute?

He climbed out of bed, and walked to the bathroom. When he got back out into the hallway, he looked down at his phone and smiled at it. In a sudden, terrible rush, I remembered what he had told me at the beginning of the tour—that he was in the talking stage with someone back home in the Bay Area, but that it wasn't anything serious yet.

I had absolutely no right to be jealous. None. Especially because I had also told him I had the same thing going on, even though it was a bold-faced lie.

"Good news?" I asked, trying to keep my voice casual.

Simon looked up at me. "Just Felix being grumpy," he said, his smile tender.

My stomach unclenched with relief. Not that it mattered, of course. I just…

"Hey, do you ever play Words With Friends?" Simon asked.

"No," I said. Then I smiled, and added, "I *win* at Words With Friends."

"Gauntlet *thrown*," Simon replied. He climbed into bed next to me while I pulled out my phone.

"Get ready to have your ass handed to you," I said.

"My ass would be honored, but that's not gonna happen."

"Your ass *would* be honored," I said.

And then we sat side by side while I beat him in Words With Friends four times in a row.

"Okay," Simon said. "My ass has been thoroughly handled tonight."

I giggled and looked over at him. "I guess that's what you get for sharing a bed with me."

Simon laughed and returned my gaze. And then he just kept…looking at me. His hazel eyes moved over my face, and I couldn't look away.

He was so handsome that it was actually startling. His still-damp hair, silky and curling. His expressive eyes. A thin layer of stubble covered his cheeks and jaw. I suddenly longed to know how it felt against my skin.

"We should probably go to bed," he said quietly. My eyes were drawn to his lips for a moment as he spoke, and something inside of me leaned forward.

"We are in bed," I replied. I tried to keep the tremor out of my voice.

Simon's lips curled into a soft smile. "I mean to sleep," he said. "It's almost 4 am."

I could see his pulse thudding gently at a spot along his neck, and I wanted to lean forward and press my lips there. I was suddenly deeply aware of how good he smelled, how the heat from his skin made my whole body hum. I swallowed.

"That's probably a good idea."

Simon looked at me for another long moment, then climbed out of bed to turn the light off. The room was plunged into almost total darkness.

"Holy shit," he said from across the room. "I can't see shit."

I laughed and turned on my phone flashlight. "Here," I said. I lit the way for Simon to crawl into bed beside me. We both scooted down and settled into our (separate) blankets.

I had no idea how I was going to be able to sleep tonight. He was right there. *Right there.* I wanted to lick him from head to toe and then tell him how adorable he was. Fuck the Oregon Rule.

I mean, if he was even interested in me.

"Hey, Simon?" I asked.

"Yeah?" His voice was low and sleepy. It made me want to scoot closer, lean my head on his shoulder, wrap an arm around his ribs.

"What's she like?"

"What's who like?"

"The girl back home," I whispered. "The one you're talking to."

Simon was quiet for so long that I was certain he'd fallen asleep, but then I heard him shift in the bed. "We stopped talking."

My heart zoomed from my chest down to my toes, then up into my head, before finally settling, thudding hard, back in my center. Relief and despair all at once.

"Then what *was* she like?" I finally managed. "Not that she's like, dead, or something. Unless she is, then—"

"She's not dead," Simon whispered, a smile in his voice.

I shifted so that I was lying on my back. I could barely bring myself to ask the next question. "So what was she like? What kind of girl is the rock god Simon Burroughs interested in?"

"Rock god, huh?"

"Come on."

Simon was quiet for another long moment. Then I heard him whisper, "Someone interesting." Another pause. "Rebellious. Good vocabulary. Talented. Pretty…"

A few seconds later, Simon was snoring.

I smiled in the darkness.

CHAPTER 10

The Make Out Playlist

JULY 15: CRESCENT CITY, CALIFORNIA TO COOS BAY, OREGON

SIMON

When I woke up the next morning, it was to find that somehow, in the night, I'd gathered Marlowe into my arms.

Marlowe was facing away from me, snoring softly. The smell of her, warm and feminine, surrounded me. I had one arm thrown over her waist, tucking her whole body into mine. Her butt was pressed up against my crotch, and if she were awake, she would feel the effect she was having on me. I had no idea where either of our blankets were.

I swallowed. I really didn't want to let go of her, but consent felt a little dubious in this situation. I was definitely spooning her without her permission, but I also didn't do it on purpose. Either way, I had a situation in my sweatpants to contend with. So it was probably best that I get up and get into the shower. Take care of this situation by jerking off real quick.

Again.

Because it turned out that a barely dressed Marlowe,

wearing my boxers in our shared bed, was a little too much for me last night. A man has his limits. So I took my aching cock in my hand under the shower water in an effort to get my raging hormones under control. It…sort of worked. I was at least able to see, think, and talk straight for the rest of the night.

I slowly withdrew my arm from around Marlowe's waist, then turned so that I was laying on my back. I glanced down at my sweats, where I was pitching a truly impressive tent. I started to roll over so that I could climb out of bed when I felt an arm wrap around me. I froze. Marlowe had turned toward me in her sleep. She threw a leg over one of mine and nuzzled her head into my chest. She was snoring again within seconds.

I had to get out of this bed before I combusted. Because her strong thigh was inches away from my erection and what I really wanted was to wake her up and pull her on top of me, then grab handfuls of her ass while she rode my dick.

And that would *definitely* be breaking the Oregon Rule.

I slowly, slowly slid out from under her weight, praying to god I wouldn't wake her. I ended up on my hands and knees on the floor, where I stayed for a full thirty seconds, listening tensely. If she woke up right now, I would have two questions to answer: why are you on the floor like that and why are you completely bricked? Finally, I heard Marlowe shift, then resume snoring.

When I finally made it to the bathroom, I practically tore my clothes off. Under the hot water of the shower, I took my cock in my hand, feeling slightly crazed. I thought of Marlowe in the bed, the warmth of her, the weight of her. My hands moved fast. I stroked myself, leaning against the shower wall in my desperation. I thought of Marlowe's deep red lips, her deep blue eyes, the way she moved her fingers when she played guitar.

I remembered how it felt to have my arms around her. The feeling of *her* arm flung over me in the bed. Her perfect ass tucked against me. I imagined her rolling her hips in that position, and had to stifle a moan. If we were in bed like that together, if there was nothing between us, I could thrust into her from behind while I reached around and held her tits. I could imagine the feel of her hard nipples in my palms. The aching heat in me was growing, and I pumped myself faster.

I felt a tightening low in my stomach, and within seconds I was hissing out my release. I leaned my head against the wall, my chest heaving.

"Goddamn," I whispered.

When I made my way out of the bathroom, Marlowe was sitting up in bed, looking at her phone. Her hair was messy, and I could see the crease of the pillow across one cheek. The sight made something inside of me swell with tenderness.

"Morning," she said, giving me a soft smile.

"Morning," I replied. I cleared my throat. "There's an extra towel for you in there if you want to shower."

"Thanks."

We looked at each other for a moment. I wondered if she was aware of our accidental cuddling in the night.

"Sorry if I snored," she finally said.

"I didn't notice," I lied.

The rest of the morning was spent in friendly banter over breakfast and while packing up, and I decided that if Marlowe didn't mention our morning spooning session, I wouldn't either. We hugged Chloe and Emery, and then we were on our way to Coos Bay.

I didn't think it would be possible with Marlowe in the

driver's seat next to me, but I fell asleep almost immediately. When I opened my eyes, Marlowe was humming along softly with the music she had playing. Her dark brown hair looked soft and touchable, her eyes dreamy.

"Hey," I said.

Marlowe glanced over at me. "Hey," she said, smiling.

"How long was I asleep?"

"Hour and a half or so?"

I glanced out the window at the coast to the west of us, the Pacific stretching out into the distance outside of Marlowe's window. I was shocked I could relax enough to fall asleep.

"Did I snore?" I asked.

She shook her head, then reached over and patted my thigh. "Pick some tunes for us," she said. "I'm tired of listening to mine. What playlists have you got?"

I opened my phone to my playlists, reading them aloud in my half-awake state. "Uh…chill vibes, party mix, get it playlist…"

"What's a 'get it playlist'?" Marlowe asked.

I cleared my throat. I was suddenly much more awake. "It's my um…you know, *the* playlist. 'Get it' as in 'get it on.'" Marlowe grinned at me. "I used to call it the 'Make Out and More Mixtape,'" I added.

"We should listen to that one!"

I looked over at Marlowe, whose grin had widened.

I blinked at her. "You want to listen to my make out playlist?"

"Hell yeah."

"Well, it's…I dunno, it feels weird to just…listen to it. And not do anything else."

Marlowe hit her turn signal and made her way to the side of the road.

Then stopped the car.

Wait. What? What was happening.

My heart was hammering in my chest, and I was suddenly finding it very hard to breathe. I felt a heat low in my belly. I swallowed hard.

When I turned to look at Marlowe, she was reaching forward to adjust something on the dashboard. She glanced at me. "The car has to be stopped for the Bluetooth to connect to a new device," she said.

Oh.

Right.

"Yeah," I said. Once my phone was connected, I pressed play and the first snap/tongue click rhythm of Janelle Monae's "Make Me Feel" filled the car.

"Mmm, absolutely," Marlowe said, merging back onto the road.

My skin felt very aware of the way Marlowe had just said "mmm" but I probably shouldn't think about that.

"This isn't totally fair," I said after a while.

"Why not?"

"Because these are my…private time songs, and you're hearing what they are, and I don't know what yours are."

I caught Marlowe smiling at me. "'Private time songs,' huh?" she teased. "Fine, for every one of your songs we play, I'll tell you one of mine and you can look it up and play it."

"So you have a make out playlist, too?"

"Of course I have a make out playlist," Marlowe said. "I'm a musician."

I looked out the window as Janelle Monae's voice filled the car. Now and then, Marlowe sang along. When it was done, I turned to her.

"Your turn."

"'Let's Take a Walk' by Raphael Saadiq," Marlowe said.

"I don't know it. Why this one?" I asked while I was pulling it up.

"Because one time I took a walk with this guy and then we made out in his car for like two hours."

I almost said, "Lucky guy," but caught myself before it slipped out.

"You and your walks," is what I did say. "Weird walks, make out walks." The song was great—an upbeat tune with these lyrics about bodies being wet and the room being too loud so whaddaya say we get out of here?

Maybe this was a terrible idea. Because all I could do was picture making out with Marlowe while we listened to these songs. Subject change needed. I turned to her.

"Did you always know you wanted to play music?" I asked.

Marlowe nodded. "For as long as I can remember. It wasn't until I was a teenager that I even realized that it was kind of unusual for girls to be rock stars, but I literally never cared. I got my first electric guitar when I was fourteen and never looked back."

"Please never look back," I said.

Marlowe threw a smile in my direction, and it felt like sunshine injected straight into my veins.

CHAPTER 11
Is This Boyhood?
JULY 15: COOS BAY, OREGON

Simon gazed out of the front window, watching the scenery. (That gorgeous profile.)

"What about you?" I asked. "Did you always want to do music?"

"I've always *loved* music," he replied. "When I was little, I used to want to be a writer. I still think about it sometimes. I'd like to write about music, actually. If I ever got tired of making it myself."

"Do you write songs for the Boy Scouts?"

He nodded. "It's me and Felix, mostly. Sometimes Aaron or Wendy will throw something in. They're all really good at taking something I've written and making it better."

"We should play the trees song for a show," I said, smiling.

Simon turned to me. "The one we all made up in the Redwoods?"

"That one."

"Holy shit, that's a brilliant idea," he said. "Who writes the songs for Queen Anne?"

"That's 99% Jem," I said. "When we first started, she wrote with an iron fist. Didn't let anyone change anything. But she's relaxed a lot over the years. Things are more collaborative now."

We were both quiet for a minute. "Let's Take A Walk" finished playing, and Simon looked down at his phone. The chunky opening chords of Pearl Jam's "In the Moonlight" came on over the car speakers.

Dear lord, Simon had good taste in make out music. I didn't know what the hell I was thinking, suggesting that we listen to these songs. My whole body had been tingling since that first one. Because apparently, I had never wanted anything as much as I wanted to make out with Simon to this music. We had to keep talking or I was gonna end up pulling over and breaking the Oregon Rule.

"When you write a song, do you go in knowing what it's going to be about, or do you just sort of follow your instincts?" I asked.

"Both," Simon replied. "Not at the same time, but for some songs, I have a really specific theme or idea in mind. Other times, I'm just messing around and something makes its way to the surface. And it's almost always something interesting. I've learned to trust my instincts and just, like…follow where the muse leads me."

I glanced over to see him smiling softly. God, I was such a sucker for creative boys. I thought back to my worry about Simon turning out to be either really boring or really misogynistic. It turned out he was neither—he was funny and creative and endearingly square, a guy who wrote great music and took pictures of cool things in venue bathrooms. Yes, the Oregon Rule had been on my mind a lot on this tour. But Simon was also making his way into the friendly parts of my heart. I liked hanging out with him. How had we only known each other for a week and a half?

"What are you thinking about?" Simon said.

I looked at him briefly. "Friendship," I replied.

"What about friendship?"

I thought. Then I decided to tell half of the truth. "I'm glad we're becoming friends," I said.

"Same," Simon replied. I didn't even have to look over at him to know he was smiling when he said it.

We spent the rest of the drive taking turns with song suggestions and watching the scenery. When we pulled into the parking lot for Horsfall Beach, Jem's car and the boys' van were parked next to each other. They must have just arrived, too, because everyone was stretching as they climbed out of the vehicles. I pulled up next to them and rolled down my window. "Greetings and salutations!" I called out.

"Hey, you're here!" Ducky said. She paused. "What... is going on in your car?"

I frowned at her, and then realized that Marvin Gaye's "Let's Get It On" was blaring from my speakers. I laughed.

"Don't worry about it," I said. I turned the car off and climbed out.

The wind whipped my hair around, and goosebumps rose on my arms. It was mid-July, but the Oregon Coast isn't exactly known for its warm beaches. I walked around to the trunk to grab a hoodie out of my duffel.

Or, to be more specific, to grab Simon's hoodie. He came around to the trunk to grab something from his bag. I caught his eye as I pulled the sweater over my head. "If you ever want this back..."

"You can wear it," he finished.

"Oh. I was going to say that I'm never giving it to you."

Simon laughed and stepped toward me. "That's also not a problem," he said softly. "It looks good on you." He ran his hands down my arms.

It was so intimate, so unexpected. This was flirting, right? Simon was flirting with me? I looked up into his warm gaze.

I don't know how long we would have stood like that if Ducky hadn't interrupted. "How long do you boys have until you have to leave?"

Simon stepped away from me. "It's a 3-hour drive to Lincoln City, but sound check isn't until like 9 pm, so we've got pretty much all day."

"Time enough to find some kick-ass rocks, then."

"Hell yeah, kick-ass rocks!" I replied, then followed Ducky onto the beach.

As soon as we hit the sand, I yanked off my shoes and ran straight for the ocean. It was completely freezing, like the Pacific always is in this part of the world. The others came and joined me, and half of us spent a few minutes screaming as the waves washed over our bare feet, running away, then running back.

Wendy picked up a handful of kelp from the wet sand. "Should I eat this?" he asked.

Simon reached out and plucked it from his hand. "No, you shouldn't eat that!"

"Isn't it just seaweed?" Aaron asked.

"No," Simon told him. "And even if it was, you shouldn't eat it straight off the beach."

Out of the corner of my eye, I saw Felix and Rose walking slowly along the shore, talking quietly. Honestly, I didn't blame them. The rest of us were kind of chaotic. Jem was sitting in the dry sand close to the parking lot, looking down at her phone.

"Log!" Aaron shouted. I watched as Simon, Aaron,

and Wendy all surrounded a massive log that was in the process of washing up onto the sand. Aaron moved to one end and attempted to lift it, and when he couldn't do it, Simon and Wendy joined him.

I made my way to where the sand was dryer and sat down, letting it run through my fingers. The boys successfully rolled the log out of the water, and it soon became clear that the boys' goal was to make the log stand upright. I couldn't help but smile watching them.

Ducky sat down next to me. "Cool-ass rock," she said and deposited a damp stone into my hand. It was dark gray, shot through with glittering white quartz.

"This is a great rock," I replied, studying it and handing it back to her.

I heard Wendy yell, "No! From this side!" We watched Simon, Aaron, and Wendy all struggle with the log. They clearly didn't have a plan, but damn did they have determination.

"Is this boyhood?" I asked.

Ducky smiled. "May toxic masculinity never find them."

We watched them in silence for a few moments. Then Ducky nudged my shoulder, speaking quietly. "Hey. Maybe cool it with Simon, yeah?"

I turned to her, my stomach dropping. "What do you mean?" I asked.

"Oregon Rule," she replied.

"Nothing's going on with me and Simon," I said. And I was pretty sure that was true. Because nothing *could* happen with me and Simon.

"Marlowe. You're wearing his hoodie."

I rolled my eyes. "It was still in my bag."

"Okay," Ducky said. But she said it like she didn't believe me.

"I swear. Nothing's going on."

"I said okay." She paused, gazing out at the guys, still struggling to push the log upright. "I mean, I wouldn't blame you if you were into him. He's like if Ryan Gosling and Lord Byron had a baby."

I laughed. "That's…true, actually."

Ducky studied me. "And the two of you did spend the night together last night. Did anything…happen?"

I thought of Simon and me last night, playing Words With Friends in the same bed, me wearing his boxer shorts, the heat of him next to me. His words as he fell asleep.

"Nothing happened," I said, truthfully. I looked out at the boys, just in time to see them step away from the log, leaving it perfectly balanced on its end. All three of them raised their arms and cheered. "Good job!" I called out.

"You know I love you," Ducky said. She took my hand. "I just don't want you to get hurt. And I also don't want you guys to break the Oregon Rule and fuck up the tour."

I turned to her and saw so much sincere friendship in her face that my heart melted. How could I possibly risk this kind of friendship for a guy? Even if the guy was really great? "I love you, too," I said. I squeezed her hand. "Don't worry about me. I'm not going to fuck anything up."

"Good," Ducky nodded. "Don't throw away your chance at playing Sasquatch Music Festival for some dick. No matter how good the dick is."

"Sasquatch over dick, always," I replied.

"'Sasquatch over dick' sounds like a British breakfast dish."

I burst out laughing.

"Just out of curiosity," Ducky said, her gaze drifting back to the boys. "What *would* you do if there was no Oregon Rule?"

I dared to steal a glance at Simon, who was now attempting to knock the log back over with Aaron and Wendy by throwing sticks and rocks at it. I truly didn't want Ducky to worry about me.

"Nothing," I said. "I'm not interested in him."

I stood, then made my way over to the boys and their log, picking up a stick on the way.

CHAPTER 12

From Lincoln City, With Love

JULY 17: LINCOLN CITY, OREGON

SIMON

I spent all day yesterday wishing Marlowe was here with us, so that we could go on a weird walk together. It wasn't quite the same doing it by myself. (I could say that about a lot of things, honestly…) The boys and I had the whole day free, and I resisted texting Marlowe the entire time. Maybe it was probably good to have a break. Let my lust cool off a little.

So I have no idea why I spent part of the day yesterday writing a song about how much I wanted Marlowe. I didn't *intend* to do that—I was just kind of messing around on the guitar, but then apparently my subconscious took over. The boys were all there in the motel room, so I kept the lyrics as vague as possible. But when Felix heard what I was doing, he pulled out his keyboard and joined in, and then Aaron got his bass and Wendy started using his sticks on the back of a chair, and then suddenly we were writing a new Boy Scouts of Atlantis song.

About Marlowe.

Writing a song about someone you're on tour with wasn't even close to breaking the Oregon Rule. But if the other guys—especially Felix—knew, they would probably tell me I was playing with fire.

But the song was good enough that we decided to try doing it at our next show. We were playing the tiniest venues in the tiniest towns for most of this tour, but there was something kind of fun about that. It meant we could do things like play a song that we just wrote that afternoon at sound check, with a plan to play it again for a bunch of drunk tourists. We were fourth out of six bands on the schedule, so even if we crashed and burned, the audience would probably be forgiving.

I gave myself until after the first band finished before I finally pulled out my phone and texted Marlowe.

> ME: How's Corvalis? Have you gone on a weird walk yet?

Marlowe just replied with a picture of a man standing in line at a grocery store, holding a live chicken.

> ME: Was she for sale?

Marlowe "ha ha'd" my comment, then replied.

> MARLOWE: This one is actually layers of weird, because the man was BUYING CHICKEN

> MARLOWE: Like, dead chicken

> MARLOWE: Chicken breasts

My stomach swooped. If ever there was evidence for how much I needed to calm the hell down about

Marlowe, it was my reaction to her typing the word "breasts."

> ME: I went on a weird walk in Lincoln City yesterday, but I didn't see anything weird

> MARLOWE: Look harder, bitch

> ME: I don't know how much harder I could have been

Oh. Wait. Uh.

How…the hell did my brain even do that? How did my fingers type that out? I watched as three dots appeared on my screen. Then disappeared.

In a flash of what I could only call divine intervention, I figured out a solution.

> ME: *looking

> ME: Sent too early lol

It was a torturous few seconds before Marlowe replied with a laughing emoji. I stood in a corner of the bar, nodding along to the band onstage, waiting for her to say something more.

> MARLOWE: I was about to ask what the hell was going on in Lincoln City

Thank god.

> MARLOWE: Have you guys already played?

> ME: We're on in twenty minutes or so

MARLOWE: Time for you to work some
magic, Simon

I didn't understand how that could be so hot. The fact
that she thought I had magic to work. The way she used
my name. I felt someone grab my arm, and turned to see
Aaron by my side.

"Felix wants us backstage," he said. I typed out one
final text to Marlowe.

ME: Alakazam

Then I followed Aaron backstage.

I BARELY GOT OFFSTAGE after our set before I pulled my
phone out again. I felt like an addict. I needed another hit
of my new favorite drug, the one with stunning blue eyes
and a great sense of humor.

ME: We just played a new song that we
wrote literally this afternoon and it went
awesome

MARLOWE: A Christmas (in July) miracle!

I paused. Then typed out a response.

ME: This is something you should know
about me. I actually hate Christmas

MARLOWE: What kind of monster hates
Christmas???

ME: *growls*

MARLOWE: Why though???

ME: Because it's cold and consumerist!

"Hi!" a voice said.

I looked up to see a woman about my age smiling up at me. She was…well, she was actually adorable. I doubt she was even five feet tall, and she had mischievous dark eyes and a blonde pixie cut.

"Hi," I said.

She leaned toward me so that she could be heard over the music. "That was a great set!"

"Thanks!"

"Are you guys in town long?"

"We head to Corvalis in the morning," I replied.

"Too bad," she replied. "I'm Cami, by the way." She held out her hand and I shook it.

"Nice to meet you. I'm Simon."

I was trying to figure out what she meant by "too bad" that we weren't staying in town long, but then she reached out and placed a hand squarely on my chest.

"Some friends and I are gonna go to another bar after this," she said. She lowered her head slightly and looked up at me through long lashes. "Do you want to come?"

"Oh. Uh."

I was aware of my hands hanging awkwardly by my sides. What were you supposed to do when a cute girl put her hand on your chest? Put one of your hands over it? Step forward and wrap your arms around her?

Also, did I want to come with her and her friends to another bar?

I knew where this night could go. The Oregon Rule didn't apply to audience members at shows. I definitely couldn't bring her back to the motel room, but if she was a local, I'm sure I could go to her place.

Did I want to?

I looked down at Cami while my thoughts swirled. Maybe it would be good for me. To be with someone else. Get Marlowe out of my mind. Maybe a quick hookup with a stranger would…scratch the itch, so to speak.

But then my eyes dropped to Cami's lips, and I just… couldn't imagine it. Couldn't imagine kissing her, touching her. The thought did almost nothing for me.

My phone buzzed in my pocket, the persistent pulse of an incoming call. I pulled it out and saw Marlowe's name on the screen. My blood fizzed with happiness.

"Sorry, I've got to take this," I said. I walked outside and answered the call.

"Hey," I said.

"Hey," Marlowe replied. "How was your set?"

"Fun," I replied. "The new song went…surprisingly well. Considering it was barely written."

"I wanna hear it in Corvalis!"

I swallowed. "Yeah."

The door behind me opened, and Cami and a handful of her friends walked out. She caught my eye, and then came over to touch my arm.

"We're heading to that bar now. You coming?"

I pulled my phone away from my ear and shook my head. "Sorry, no thanks. Have a good time!" I brought my phone back to my ear. "Sorry about that."

"Who was that?" Marlowe teased.

"Um, an audience member invited us to another bar for drinks."

"Invited *all* of you or invited *you*?"

I watched Cami and her friends walk away. "Um…me?"

"Why didn't you go?"

Something in her voice made my breath catch. Maybe I was imagining it, but there was a sincerity to her question that, I dunno, surprised me.

I shrugged, even though she couldn't see me. "Didn't feel like it," I replied.

"The Oregon Rule doesn't apply to audience members." That teasing tone had returned to Marlowe's voice.

"Wasn't interested."

Marlowe was quiet for so long that I glanced at the screen to make sure the call was still connected.

"Marlowe?" I asked.

"What would happen if you broke the Oregon Rule?"

My blood seemed to speed up in my veins. "I uh...I don't actually know, since it's never happened before," I said. "Felix would probably get pissed. Maybe everyone would."

"It's *never* happened before?"

"Well, none of the boys in the Boy Scouts of Atlantis are gay, so we don't have to worry about dating each other and ruining things."

"...And dating tour mates?"

I tried to breathe normally. "I don't—" My voice cracked, and I took a moment to clear my throat. "I don't think it would break up the band, necessarily." It took every ounce of will power I had to add, "Probably still not a great idea, though."

"Right," Marlowe said. She paused before saying, "Okay, tell me more about Lincoln City."

CHAPTER 13

Siren Song

JULY 19: CORVALLIS, OREGON

MARLOWE

I saw Simon look up from his guitar right as Ducky yelled "Reunited, baby!" I followed her inside. An unfamiliar melody floated through the air.

Simon and I's eyes met, and I felt a zap of electricity hum through me. How was he even better-looking than I remembered? It had only been four days. I waved, and he paused his guitar playing to wave back and smile at me.

"Reunited, and with a new song!" Aaron replied.

"You guys wrote a whole song while you were in Lincoln City?" Jem asked, setting her amp down.

Simon shrugged. "It's still a little rough, but we played it last night and it went pretty good."

"If you guys are doing that," I said, "Then I say we all play the trees song together."

"That's not polished enough at all," Felix replied.

"We could treat it as a jam song," Rose said. She tilted her head to look at the rest of us.

"Are we *all* playing on it?" Felix asked. He glanced around the stage. "There isn't enough room for all of us."

"I'll just sing," I said. "So we don't have as many guitars."

"Same," Jem added.

"And two basses is awesome," Aaron said.

"Do Ducky and me have to fight it out about drums?" Wendy asked.

"Waaaaaaaiiiiiitt!" Ducky yelled as she ran outside. In four seconds, she came sprinting back in, a tambourine in her hand. She grinned at us. "I'm ready!"

Felix sighed. "Fine," he said. "We can run it at the end of this sound check, but if it sucks, we skip it."

"Deal," I said.

The boys had finished their sound check, and they hung around while we did ours, and it took everything in me to not stare at Simon the whole time. He was so *hot*. You would think I would be used to it by now. But nope. That stubbled jawline and those curls and those eyes. Damn.

Running the trees song was chaotic but so much fun that Felix gave it his stamp of approval. Rose grinned at him and then high fived me.

OUR SET WAS GOOD—NOTHING extraordinary, but nothing awful either. But the boys were on fire. I don't know what happened to them in Lincoln City. Rose, Ducky, Jem, and I were all jumping around like crazy in front of the stage.

I'd learned by now that there were sort of two Simons —or really, two sides of the same Simon. Simon offstage was sweet and a little anxious and artsy. Simon onstage was violently, aggressively hot. It's like he had this presence that he could just turn on, and he could turn everyone else in the room on with it. The way he tilted his hips until his heels lifted off the ground, the way his jaw tightened when he was singing hard, his fingers moving over the neck of his guitar while his dark curls fell into his eyes…all of it was hypnotizing.

I stood in the audience, looking up at him, and trying not to make it too obvious that I wanted to unhinge my jaw and swallow him whole. A weird part of me thought that maybe I should watch the other members of the band too, just to like, even it out somehow? Avoid being too suspicious. But when Simon played or sang, I could not tear my eyes away from him. He had a complete hold on me.

The boys finished a song and Simon flashed a smile out at the crowd. For a brief moment, I felt a swell of possessive pride. How many girls in this room were swooning at the lead singer up there? And I *knew* him. *Personally*. I'd worn his boxers while we slept in the same bed.

I watched him turn back to Felix, and the two mouthed a few things at each other. Then Simon turned back to the mic.

"You all have been an amazing crowd. We're going to close out with a new one." He turned to the guys behind him. "Unless we crash and burn, in which case, we'll play something else to redeem ourselves."

"We won't crash and burn!" Aaron yelled.

"Okay," Simon grinned. He moved his hands over the frets, a piercing melody singing out. It was slow and dangerous-sounding…almost haunting. He kept playing and…

Holy shit. Holy *fuck*. This was the hottest song I'd ever heard in my life. My hips started swaying almost of their

own accord. I tilted my head back, closed my eyes and let
the music wash over me.

Her siren song
I'm all at sea
She's calling me
I know it's wrong
My sailor's thoughts
All tied in knots

Her aching melody floats through the air
Wrapping my thoughts up in her long dark hair
I see flashing lights in blue and red
Visions of her dancing through my head
Pulling me down
Pulling me down

Oh god.

Her siren song
Lorelei
With piercing eyes
They say it's wrong
Call me a fool
For hating rules

Her smile cuts like needles under my skin
I can't help but sigh while my heart's drownin'
She presses her lips against all of my locks
While my body gets wrecked upon the rocks
Pulling me down
Pulling me down

I stared up at Simon.

I wanted to know why he'd written this song. What it was about. Who it was about. But I wasn't sure if I could handle the answers. How had he put it into words so perfectly? All the desperate ache I felt for him? The hunger that coursed under my skin?

All of these questions were burning through me when he caught my gaze. And held it.

Breaking me down
Breaking me up
Breaking me down
Breaking me up
I give up I give in
She can be my sin
The temptation is cruel
I will break all the rules
For her

I wasn't going to survive this. I bit my lip, and watched as Simon's chest moved up and down, gasping for breath while he sang. He didn't look away, and suddenly it felt like he was singing directly *to* me. I was made of vibrating glass. I had a feeling that if he so much as touched me, I would explode.

Simon finished the stanza he was singing and then screamed into the mic, and I screamed along with him.

Whenever I saw videos of women and girls screaming at Beatles concerts, or at Elvis Presley's hips or whatever, I always "got" it. Sometimes music just fills you with so much feeling that you have to let it out. But I had never in my life felt as much as I did when Simon played that song.

The entire crowd went insane, and it was pretty damn clear that the Boy Scouts of Atlantis would not need to play another song to "redeem" themselves.

Simon gave the room a crooked smile, and I almost passed out.

"You've all been a great crowd, thank you so much," Simon said. He looked down at me and grinned. "We want to invite our tour mates, Queen Anne onstage, to join us in this next song."

I could have walked around to the steps, but Simon slung his guitar around his back and held his hand out to me. I grabbed it and let him pull me onstage.

During sound check, there weren't enough mics for all of us, so Jem and I had to just kind of stand nearby and sing along. I was planning on doing that same thing, but Simon lowered his mic stand so that I could reach it. Jem was plugging her own mic in on the other side of the stage. While everyone else was setting up, Simon turned to the crowd.

"How many of you have been out to the Redwoods in California?"

A few cheers went up from the crowd.

"For those who haven't seen those trees, they're really fucking big. And we were all really impressed with them, so we wrote a song about it."

Simon went through the intro, and then leaned in toward the mic. "*The trees here are too fucking big*," he sang. Jem and I joined in with a harmony on the second line. I leaned into the mic, my lips inches away from Simon's. The chorus was literally us just singing the same line four times in a row, and standing so close to Simon onstage, I could barely breathe well enough to sing.

I stepped away from the mic to let Simon and Jem alternate on the verse lines.

"*I thought I knew what trees were*," Simon sang.

"*But I did not know shit*," Jem added.

"*These trees are bigger than my ex's ego*."

"*And that man was not the tits.*"

"Everybody sing along!" Simon shouted.

I leaned into the mic to sing the chorus again. But after two more stanzas, we were almost drowned out by the audience singing at the top of their lungs.

From behind us, I could hear Felix joining in. Ducky shook her tambourine, and I could hear Aaron and Rose playing complimentary bass lines. I caught Simon's eye, and the two of us smiled at each other as we kept singing.

This, I thought. *This is why I love music.* I was onstage with a bunch of friends and we were singing a stupid song we made up about trees, and a bunch of strangers were singing along, and just for this moment, nothing else was important. We were together and we were making something and we were connected. Moments like this made me feel like I was right where I was supposed to be.

It was like we created these temporary little families, or villages, or something, at every show. And it could never be recreated. Every audience was different, every venue was different. You could play the exact same set two nights in a row, and it would be a completely different show—there were so many variables that made every show unique.

And right then, in a bar in Corvallis, Oregon, I was singing about trees with a bunch of friends and an audience, and it was right where all of us belonged.

CHAPTER 14

The Greenroom

JULY 20: SALEM, OREGON

SIMON

Marlowe stopped walking right in front of me, and when I looked up, I could see why. "Wow," I said.

"Someone should start an Instagram of venue greenrooms," Ducky said, looking around us. We were walking into a nine by nine foot room, with the most disgusting, acrid green wallpaper I'd ever seen in my life. Couches from the 70s lined two walls, and a handful of dirty mirrors hung haphazardly above them. There was a beanbag and a recliner, and a glass coffee table sat in the middle of all of it.

I plopped onto the couch and pulled my phone out. "It's not a venue bathroom, but this wallpaper deserves… acknowledging." I snapped a photo and posted it to my Instagram story.

Marlowe fell into the seat beside me on the couch, and my stomach did a joyful little flip. *Calm down*, I told myself. *Oregon Rule.*

It was just that she was wearing these tiny shorts and

these fishnet tights and boots that went all the way up over her knees. She'd ripped the sleeves off of an old ruffled tuxedo shirt, and she was wearing suspenders that made me very aware of how *not* flat-chested she was. Marlowe looked like every impossibly cool girl I had ever had a crush on ever.

Felix pulled out a notebook and started writing out a set list. Rose and Aaron started debating four-string vs. five-string basses. Everyone else settled into scrolling on their phones, while I concentrated really hard on not putting my arm around Marlowe next to me.

Suddenly, Jem stood up, staring down at her phone. "Holy shit!" she yelled.

"What?" Rose asked, looking concerned.

Jem stared up at us with wide eyes. "Bumbershoot is coming," she said.

The room was silent. Wendy was the first to speak. "What…does that sentence mean?"

Felix stood. "'Bumbershoot'?" he asked. "As in 'Seattle Music Festival Bumbershoot'?"

Jem nodded.

"…How?" I asked. "When?"

"I emailed a promoter," she replied. "Like, months ago. I gave her our tour schedule and told her that if she was in the area, she should come see us play. She just emailed back. She's coming to the Santa Cruz show in two weeks." Jem held her phone up to show us her screen.

This news hung in the air for two seconds, and then all of us erupted into cheers.

"That's amazing!" Ducky screamed, hugging Jem, who looked both stunned and elated.

"What do we do?" Rose asked, looking vaguely terrified.

"What do you mean, what do we do?!" Ducky replied. "We play our butts off! Tonight and in Santa Cruz!"

Jem glanced over at Felix. "I told them about you guys, too. I sent them a link to your Spotify."

I rarely saw Felix grin, but now he was beaming.

"I don't think I've ever seen all of your teeth at once, man," Aaron said.

The sound guy stuck his head in the doorway. "Boy Scouts of Atlantis, y'all ready?"

"Hell yes!" Aaron shouted, striding toward the door.

I saw Rose offer Felix a small, genuine smile, and Wendy was too busy spinning his drumsticks happily to notice anything. Jem followed, heading out to the floor with the other members of Queen Anne while the boys headed onstage. I was about to leave when Marlowe grabbed my arm.

"Wait, hang on, your tie's all crooked," she said. I turned to her so that she could reach up to adjust the knot of the tie at my throat.

"Bumbershoot," she grinned up at me.

"Bumbershoot," I replied.

Marlowe stood close, concentrating on my tie, and suddenly I felt something between us shift. Like the air had been let out of the room and now it was humming with some unnamed thing. I could feel the slight heat of her fingers, close to my chest. I was suddenly deeply aware of how close we were standing, how alone we were. I swallowed, and watched Marlowe as she watched the movement at my throat. I got a whiff of that distinctly Marlowe scent—something floral and sweet, and it was all I could do to keep from closing my eyes at the deliciousness of it.

Roughly ten seconds ago, all I could think about was the fact that we were going to play in front of a huge promoter, and now my entire brain and body was just filled with the awareness of this girl standing in front of me.

My tie was fixed, but Marlowe didn't let go of it. She looked up at me. We stood there, inches apart. She slowly ran her hands down the lapels of my sport coat. Feeling her palms moving down my chest like that, even with layers of clothing between us, was going to kill me.

When I whispered her name, I could hear how strangled my voice sounded.

"Marlowe."

That's all it took. She looked up into my face for one half second, and then, I don't know who started it, but instantly my lips were pressed against hers.

Finally, I thought.

She gasped into my mouth, her fingers tightening on my lapels. Marlowe's desperation matched mine, my lips moving fiercely against hers. I wanted to touch her everywhere at once, my hands moving into her hair, along her jaw, around her waist, up and down her back. Marlowe clung to my lapels, almost as if they were the only things keeping her upright.

She parted her lips to let my tongue sweep inside. I could not believe how good she felt. I wanted to fill my mouth with her, with every part of her. I needed more.

I walked us backwards until her spine hit the wall. I needed her pinned in place so that I could keep kissing her the way I wanted to. And I was pretty sure we couldn't stay upright much longer without some kind of support. But as soon as I felt her body flush against mine, it still wasn't enough. I reached down and curved my hand around the back of Marlowe's thigh, then hitched her leg over my hip. The noise she made sent me into orbit. Her fingers made their way to my scalp, running through my hair as we kissed. I almost couldn't bring myself to believe it was happening. Marlowe Wainscoate was writhing against this wall beneath me, and I had never felt anything so perfect in my life.

My lips left hers to fly down the side of her jaw and neck. I wanted to tell her that she tasted as good as she smelled, but that would require me to stop kissing her, and I really didn't want to do that.

But then suddenly, I felt her hands pressing hard against my chest, shoving me away from her. I stumbled backward, then looked up to meet her eyes.

Marlowe stared at me, her pupils blown wide. A pink flush was spread over her cheeks and neck, and I desperately wanted to know how far down her body that flush went. Her chest was heaving, both of her hands pressed flat against the wall, almost as if she was trying to hold herself up.

Her gaze dropped to the front of my pants, and I used my hands to try and cover myself, but based on the heat in her eyes, I could tell she had already seen how hard our kissing had made me. My dick was aching, *aching* for more of her.

"You have to go onstage," Marlowe gasped.

I blinked at her. I had literally forgotten about the show. The show that was happening in like, two seconds, if it wasn't already happening. Any second, Felix was going to come into this room and wonder why Marlowe and I were standing six feet apart from each other and breathing like we'd just run a marathon.

Actually, he wouldn't wonder why. He'd know.

I closed my eyes, trying to concentrate on something, anything else to get my ragingly lustful thoughts under control. "You have to leave this room," I said. "I have to… you have to leave this room." I opened my eyes just enough to see whether or not she was gone.

She wasn't. Instead, she was standing there, her eyes so damn blue and her skin so damn soft that all I could think about was kissing her again, and that could not happen.

"I gotta go onstage," I managed.

"Wait, your hair…" Marlowe said. She took a step forward, reaching out to fix what I'm sure was a mess on the top of my head. But I held up my hand in a panicked gesture.

"If you touch my hair, this will never…" I gestured vaguely at my pants. Marlowe bit her lip, and my gaze dropped to her mouth. "And if you keep looking at me like that, that will also…I will never…I have to get onstage."

Marlowe took a step backward, then smoothed a hand over her clothes. She nodded and walked out of the room.

I stood there, watching her go, the Oregon Rule in absolute shambles around me.

CHAPTER 15

I'll Be Your Seatbelt

JULY 21: SALEM, OREGON TO PORTLAND, OREGON

MARLOWE

The Boy Scouts stayed in a different motel from us last night.

And now, sitting in the car on our way to Portland, I was losing my mind.

I had already pulled out my phone to text Simon roughly two hundred times, and put it away another two hundred times without texting him.

Because I had no idea what to say.

"That was the hottest kiss of my entire life and you're all I can think about"?

"What the hell was that?"

"Do you want to keep breaking the Oregon Rule?"

Because I sure as hell wanted to keep breaking the Oregon Rule. I wanted to break the Oregon Rule until I couldn't walk anymore.

That kiss. God, that *kiss.* Just the memory of it sent my blood rushing. Simon's hands everywhere. His lips moving against mine. The way he shoved me against the wall, kissing me harder.

I stifled a moan.

The other thing that was torturing me about this situation was that I definitely could not tell Ducky. So I just sat in the driver's seat as we drove from Salem to Portland, feeling like I was going to combust and not being able to say anything about it.

Ducky picked up the walkie talkie from the console between us. "Ducky to Jem, over."

A voice came crackling over the walkie. "Go for Jem, over."

I smiled. I kind of loved the formality with which we used these walkie talkies. We didn't *have* to use "over" or any of the other walkie-talkie speak. But Jem loved rules, so we all just kind of fell into walkie-talkie speak with her.

"Did you secretly email any other festival reps? Over?" Ducky asked.

"Yes, over," Jem replied.

Oh yeah. The festival rep. I'd been so lost in thoughts of kissing Simon that I had literally forgotten about Bumbershoot.

Ducky made an exasperated noise and spoke into the walkie talkie again. "Do you want to tell us *which ones*? Over!?"

Jem's voice crackled over her reply. "Bottlerock Napa Valley, Northern Nights, and Sasquatch, but I haven't heard from anyone else. I'm going to concentrate on driving. Over and out."

Ducky and I looked at each other. "Sasquatch?!" I exclaimed.

"Fucking Sasquatch!"

"Okay, but she said they didn't get back to her," I said.

"Still," Ducky said. "Sasquatch."

I suddenly remembered Ducky's admonition in Coos Bay, to choose "Sasquatch over dick." I decided not to think too much about it.

We were staying in Portland for almost a week, so we had gotten an Airbnb. The house was delightfully Portland-y, with moss-covered brick steps and a porch with two rocking chairs. When Ducky and I pulled up, Jem and Rose were stepping out of Jem's Subaru. The boys' van wasn't here yet.

"Hey Marlowe, pick us a room," Ducky said. "Get a good one before the boys get here."

I grinned and raced up the steps to where Jem was already unlocking the door. I dashed from room to room, before ending up downstairs. This room had pale blue wallpaper, and white curtains hanging in front of a high window. In the center of the room sat a canopy bed.

"Marlowe and Ducky claim this room!" I shouted.

I was still wondering where the boys were, but I managed to distract myself by bringing in gear and then hauling bags down to the bedroom. Ducky and I had both always been kind of chaotic when it came to packing and unpacking, but I needed a minute to sort my thoughts so I opened my bag and pulled out my toiletries, setting them on the antique dressing table.

I glanced up at my reflection in the mirror.

Simon would be here any minute. We'd be staying in the same house together for the next four days. I had no idea what was going on between us, but I wanted more of him so badly it made my skin ache. I felt reckless and desperate and completely out of control. I took a deep breath.

"Cool it, Marlowe," I said.

I exited the room, and walked right into Simon. He put his hands on my upper arms to steady me.

"Hey," he said.

"Hey," I replied. A warm smile spread across his face, and it somehow made him *even more* handsome. I was deeply, deeply aware of the fact that everyone else was upstairs, and that there was a bed directly behind Simon. And another one directly behind me.

We stood there, staring at each other, and I could practically hear the air crackling around us. We had to talk about it. We had to. I finally managed to open my mouth to say something.

"Should we—"

But before I could finish, Jem's voice rang out from the top of the stairs. "Grocery run! Y'all coming?"

Simon glanced up toward Jem, then back at me. "Let's go get groceries," he said.

"Can we all fit in the van?" Aaron asked. He glanced around at the small group standing in the driveway. "One, two, three, four, five, six." His face fell. "We only have five seats."

"We can squish," I said. "It seems dumb to take two cars."

"Or one of us could stay here," Felix said.

"Nah, we can all fit," Simon said.

"Shotgun!" Rose called.

"Seat behind shotgun!" Jem added.

Felix pulled his keys out. "I'll drive."

Aaron glanced at me and Simon. "I am too big to squish," he said.

Simon walked over and hugged Aaron tight around the middle. "You're just the right size to squish," he said, his voice muffled against Aaron's chest.

"I meant in the back of the van," Aaron said. "Can you and Marlowe squish?"

Simon lifted his head from Aaron's chest and looked at me. "Whaddaya say, Marlowe?"

The idea of "squishing" into the back of the van with Simon had my imagination running wild, but…yes.

"Yes."

It turned out that there actually was a seat in the back of the van, but it was just one bucket seat—the rest had been taken out to make room for gear. Simon climbed past the first row of seats, sat down in the single seat, and called out to me. "Come on back!"

I crawled in after him, then knelt, looking around. The boys had unloaded all their gear, so there was just a big empty space back there.

"Where do I sit?"

"Anywhere," Felix said.

"Wait, what about a seatbelt?" Jem asked.

Simon stretched his arms out. "I'll be your seatbelt, Marlowe. "

I met his eyes, and what had been playful suddenly grew heated.

"Hey, Oregon Rule!" Aaron exclaimed.

For a moment, my stomach dropped. But when I looked at Aaron, he had a teasing grin on his face.

"This is about safety!" Simon retorted, returning Aaron's teasing smile. Then he looked back at me.

Was I really doing this? Was I really about to sit in Simon's lap as we drove across town? With his strong thighs beneath me and his chest and arms pressed close?

Yes, I was.

I had to put a hand on Simon's knee to bring myself up to lap-sitting height. Simon rested one arm along the window, so I settled with my back against it, my legs draped over his lap.

I didn't know what to do with my arms.

"Here," Simon said quietly. He took my arm and lifted it so that it hung around his neck. I tried not to shift against him.

"The other one," Simon said gruffly.

"What?"

"Put your other arm around me."

I swallowed, then brought my other arm up so that I could rest my hand on his shoulder. Simon's arm came around my waist, his hand spread wide on my ribs. He rested his other hand on my thighs.

My entire body was on fire.

Felix called out from the driver's seat. "Everyone ready?"

"Ready!" I said, maybe a little too loudly. We jolted forward, and Simon's hand tightened on my body.

I could barely think, but I managed to whisper, "Thanks for being my seatbelt."

"Safety first," Simon replied quietly. I turned to look at him. His face was so close that even in the dark, I could see the individual flecks of gold in his eyes. My gaze dropped to his lips, slightly parted, looking so so kissable.

I looked away. "Gotta follow the law," I whispered.

"Since when do you care about rules like seatbelt laws?" Simon murmured. His breath was hot on my skin, and the sensation of it made me clutch handfuls of his shirt. Then he brushed his nose gently along my neck, causing my eyelids to flutter closed. "Rebel girl," he murmured.

Heat flooded my core, spreading down between my legs. "Rule...following...boy," I murmured back. I could have tried to come up with a better comeback, but my brain was filled with a frantic kind of buzzing and coherent thoughts weren't exactly available to me at the moment.

Simon's hand tightened on my thigh, and I bit my lip to keep from crying out. My heart was pounding so hard I was shocked that no one else in the van could hear it. Simon leaned forward and pressed a kiss to my collarbone, and my back arched into the touch. When his teeth scraped gently along that same place, I rolled my hips in desperation.

The hand that had been clutching my thigh shifted up to stop me from moving. "Marlowe," Simon whispered. His voice sounded as tortured as I felt. "Stop moving. I can't…you're…"

"You started it," I managed.

"I know but…"

"Do you want me to get off?" I asked in a low voice.

Simon looked up at me, then gave me a mischievous grin. "Yes," he said. "But not right now in this van."

A ridiculous giggle escaped me. I clapped a hand over my mouth. Simon let out a low chuckle and loosened his grip on my body.

How were we going to survive the rest of this car ride, let alone the rest of the tour?

CHAPTER 16

Treetop Adventures

JULY 22: PORTLAND, OREGON

SIMON

I don't know how I survived the rest of that car ride with Marlowe in my lap. What the hell was I thinking? I clearly wasn't thinking. I was just…a planet falling into Marlowe's orbit whenever she was nearby. My skin wanted her skin and apparently that turned off my brain. (And turned on everything else.)

I really had mostly just wanted to keep her safe in the van, at first. I didn't want her falling over in the back or flying off my lap. But then her legs were warm on top of mine and her neck was right there and she smelled so good. When she had shifted her hips, I was a goner. (A goner with a hard-on that I had roughly five minutes to get rid of. I had never concentrated so hard on getting an erection to go down in my life.)

But I made it, and we got groceries, and I was very well-behaved for the ride home, and then we all ate dinner and went to bed, and now it was morning.

I climbed the stairs into the living room at around 11

am to discover that I was the last one awake. Everyone else was sitting around, eating cereal, chatting, scrolling their phones. Marlowe looked up at me.

Her eyes were so blue that I couldn't actually think for a moment. She was in a loose t-shirt and what had to be Ducky's pajama pants, hair messy, her face bare. I had a sudden memory of her in a T-shirt and my boxer shorts, the way she draped herself over me in the morning.

Nope, I thought.

"Hey," she said.

"Morning," I replied. I headed into the kitchen to grab a bowl of cereal.

Ducky looked up from her spot on the couch. "Hey do you guys want to go do a ropes course today?"

"What's a ropes course?" Aaron asked.

"You know, like one of those…obstacle courses," Ducky replied. "Platforms around trees. Harnesses. Monkey bars."

"I still have no idea what you mean but that sounds awesome," Aaron said.

I sighed. Aaron lived his life with zero fear. And zero sense? He just barreled through life joyfully, with no thought about what could happen. I sometimes envied him.

"That also sounds expensive," Jem said.

But Ducky shook her head. "I have a group pass thing. My cousin gave it to me a few months ago, when she heard we were going to be in Portland."

"I'm down," Wendy said. "Anyone else?"

"You are all insane," Felix said.

"Come on!" Ducky cried. "It'll be a team-building activity."

"Have fun building your team," Felix said.

But now Ducky was determined. She sat up and glared

at Felix. "You have to come. You're one of the Boy Scouts. Boy Scouts do ropes things."

"No, we don't," Felix said.

Ducky frowned at him. "We can't team build with only part of the team. We can't go unless all of us go, and I want to go."

"Me, too!" Wendy added.

"And me," Aaron said.

Felix looked up at me. I glanced over at Marlowe, who was watching the others. I shrugged. "Sure," I said.

"Fine," Felix grumbled.

"All boy scouts in!" Ducky yelled. She turned to her band mates. "Queen Anne?"

"I'll go," Rose said.

Marlowe smiled. "It sounds terrifying, but I'll go if everyone else will."

Ducky turned to Jem, who scowled. "As long as we're back in time for sound check tonight."

Ducky fist pumped the air. "I'll make the reservation!"

TREETOP ADVENTURES WAS ABOUT HALF an hour outside of town, and as soon as I got out of the van, I regretted agreeing to this. There were people way too high up in the air, wearing helmets and complicated-looking harnesses, and they were basically tightrope walking between trees.

"Whoa," Wendy said. "This is some circus shit."

I caught a glimpse of Marlowe looking up at the people above us. I had the sudden crazed urge to bury my nose in the skin of her exposed neck. I remembered how good she smelled in the car last night, how soft her skin was.

Calm down, Edward Cullen, I thought to myself.

Ducky was practically skipping her way to the check-in booth. The rest of us fell into step behind her.

I stole another glance at Marlowe next to me. "No offense," I told her, "But I think Ducky might be insane."

"Oh she's definitely insane," Marlowe replied, still staring upwards.

I wanted to reach out and take her hand. But we were surrounded by people who were not aware that we had already broken the Oregon Rule, and I didn't know if Marlowe would even want to hold my hand. We should probably talk about that kiss at some point. Or we could just kiss some more, which honestly sounded way more appealing. The Oregon Rule was already broken, so would it really be that much worse to just…keep going?

Maybe that was something to talk about *after* this terrifying "team building" activity. The guide at the check-in booth gave us all helmets, then handed us clipboards with lengthy waivers. I flipped through the pages, then looked up at my tour mates. "Are we sure about this?"

Aaron was already happily signing the form. "They wouldn't do it if it wasn't safe," he said.

Felix shook his head. "I don't know if that's totally true, dude."

Aaron looked up at the rest of us blankly. "But then… how is it legal?"

I held up the clipboard. "The waivers make it legal."

But Aaron just shrugged. And before any of us could back out, we were standing in a line with harnesses around our waists and thighs, and one by one, we were hooked up to a bunch of ropes and then told to climb the tree in front of us.

Aaron hauled his enormous frame up effortlessly, which for some reason was really annoying. Wendy got halfway up before he fell, and half of us screamed, but he landed gently in a crouch, the ropes keeping him from hitting the ground harder. He just laughed and got back up because he's apparently not human. Jem looked somehow furious, but I think she was masking her fear through just pure angry adrenaline.

Marlowe and I hung back, waiting at the end of the line. My blood pressure went up by ten points every moment we got closer to the tree. I watched Rose tremble as she scaled the trunk, gripping the handholds that had been drilled into the bark. Felix stood at the bottom swearing impressively for a full thirty seconds before yelling "fuck it" and climbing as fast as he possibly could. Ducky grinned as she made her way up, calling back to us that we should add another verse to the tree song after today. About how tall *all* trees actually were.

Then it was just Marlowe and me. She turned to face me. "I changed my mind," she said. "I don't want to do this anymore."

"I don't think I ever wanted to do this," I replied. Why did she look so stinking *cute* in her helmet? "But I'll do it if you will."

Marlowe turned and craned her neck to look up at the platform some thirty feet above us. My thoughts got all Edward Cullen-y again, so I looked up too.

It did seem absurdly high up.

"Our ancestors stopped living in trees on purpose," Marlowe said. But she stepped forward to let the guide clip some ropes onto her harness. I watched her take a deep breath, then reach her arms up to start climbing.

I hadn't realized that standing below Marlowe would give me such an incredible view of her ass. And thighs. And calves. But I couldn't...not watch her? I couldn't figure out which was more suspicious, watching her or not watching her, so I alternated between both options and probably looked even more suspicious.

But I didn't have much time to think about it because then it was my turn, and the guide was attaching ropes to my harness and giving me instructions that I absolutely did not hear. I looked up at the platform above me, which now seemed even farther away.

Seven expectant faces looked down at me. Including Marlowe's. Suddenly, my body flooded with the desire to just get closer to her. I reached up and grabbed a handhold, then pulled myself toward her.

CHAPTER 17

What Kind of Pirate Are You?!

JULY 22: PORTLAND, OREGON

MARLOWE

It actually wasn't so bad once you got to the platform. Unless you looked down, which I did for a moment while Simon was climbing up, and then I saw the ground beneath him and suddenly it felt like gravity got stronger. I quickly backed up so that I was all the way against the tree.

Next to me, Felix was grumbling. "Why don't these fucking platforms have fucking railings?"

I was asking myself the same thing.

Simon pulled himself up onto the platform nearby, a thin sheen of sweat on his face.

"You made it," I said.

He gave me a shaky smile. "What's a girl like you doing in a tree like this?" he asked.

"Damned if I know."

The guide's voice rose above our conversations. "Okay, everyone, we're moving on to the paired part of the course," she said. "To get to the next platform, you'll have to work with a partner. You can try any method of getting across you want, but if one of you falls, you both fall. So pick someone you either trust or want to trust."

In a rare moment of vulnerability, Jem grabbed Ducky's hand. "Partners," she said, her voice sounding so tight she could barely get the word out.

Aaron clapped Wendy on the back. "You and me, brother?" Rose and Felix exchanged a look and then took one step closer to each other. Leaving me and Simon.

"What do you say, do you trust me?" he asked.

"I guess I don't have a choice, do I?" I replied, smiling.

The distance to the other platform was maybe twenty feet. We'd just climbed at least thirty feet, so it shouldn't have looked as intimidating, but it did. One long rope stretched above our heads, and a series of ropes were suspended at our feet, forming a loose kind of bridge. There were five or six ropes total, close enough to each other that you could try to step on a few of them at once, but I had a feeling it would be easy to slip through them and fall to the ground. There was one shorter rope hanging down about halfway across, as a kind of anchor point.

Ducky was practically dancing with anticipation, so she stepped forward, dragging Jem beside her. The guide clipped them both to the rope above and told them to go ahead. "Just remember," the guide added. "You're connected to each other, so if one person falls, the other one will, too. Good luck."

Jem and Ducky stared at the ropes in front of them before Ducky said, "Let's just run. Fast as we can." Before Jem could agree, Ducky ran out onto the ropes, forcing Jem to follow. They actually made it about halfway before they ran out of momentum. Jem screamed as they headed toward the ground, but their harnesses kept them from landing hard. Ducky laughed as she got to her feet.

"Climb up to the next platform," the guide yelled down. She turned back to the rest of us. "Who's next?"

Rose and Felix made it to the other platform by crouching and inching across sideways, each of them holding on to the ropes below with one hand and holding on to each other with the other hand. They practically collapsed onto the platform when they reached it, but I saw them exchange a grin.

Aaron and Wendy opted for a weird Army crawl, where they both scooted along the ropes on their stomachs, one after the other. It took a hundred years, and halfway across, Wendy started yelling about rope burn, but they were almost there.

As they were nearing the opposite platform, Simon turned to me. "What's the plan?" he asked.

I looked out at Wendy and Aaron. "What if we sit down?"

I turned in time to see Simon lowering himself onto the platform, looking confused. Ugh, cutest boy on the planet. I laughed. "No, on the ropes, I mean. To get across."

"Oohhh," Simon said, his cheeks pink. "Sorry, I thought you meant…"

Dear god, he was adorable. I had the insane urge to lean forward and kiss him, just to have something to do with all the affection I was feeling. But I managed to restrain myself. Simon looked thoughtfully out at the ropes.

"What if we like…A-frame?" he suggested. "Like…go sideways the way Felix and Rose did, with one hand on the rope above, but we keep each other balanced by facing each other and pressing one hand together." He lifted his hands to demonstrate, and I put my hands in his and leaned into him.

"Yeah!" I said. "That's a good idea."

And then the guide was beckoning us forward and clipping us onto the rope above and wishing us luck.

"Ready?" Simon asked.

"Ready," I replied.

He grabbed the rope above our heads and lifted one hand. I did the same and leaned toward him. Then we stepped out onto the ropes.

We were…steadier than I thought we would be. We took another step sideways, and then I looked up at Simon and grinned.

"This is actually working," I said.

"Hell yeah it is," Simon replied.

But the closer we got to the middle, the shakier our progress got. It was easier when we were close to the platform, where there was less slack. But the farther we got, the more the ropes wobbled under our feet.

I made the mistake of looking down again, and then froze. I had to close my eyes to steady my breathing.

"Okay?" Simon asked quietly.

I nodded, keeping my eyes closed.

"Marlowe," he said.

"Hm?"

"Look at me."

I managed to crack my eyes open to see Simon's face, a few inches from mine. His eyes were calm, steady. "Just focus on me," he said. "Don't look down. Just keep your eyes on my face."

I nodded, then took a deep breath as we took another step sideways. Simon's fingers interlaced with mine above our heads. "Just hold on to me," he said.

We had almost made it halfway across when one of my feet slipped. I let out a yelp of fear, but before I could fall, one of Simon's arms wrapped hard around me. I slammed into his body, my feet still scrambling, but then I realized that Simon's other hand had grabbed the rope hanging down in the middle, holding us both up.

"Can you try…to hold…still?" Simon gritted out. His arm was straining with the task of holding us both up. His voice wasn't angry, and in a moment, I was able to reach out and grab the rope as well, steadying myself.

"That was…amazing," I gasped out. My chest was pressed against Simon's, his arm still encircling me. I looked up into his face to find him smiling down at me.

"I feel like a pirate," he said.

All of the nervousness I had felt about our near miss melted away, and I burst into laughter. "How?"

"Like I just rescued a maiden who was about to fall from the rigging of a ship!"

That same urge to kiss him swelled up inside of me again, only this time I was very aware of all six of our bandmates watching us. "Let's steer this ship to the harbor, captain," I said.

"Aye aye, matey," Simon replied.

I stifled another laugh, then glanced over at the platform. "How are we going to do this?" I asked.

Simon followed my gaze, then looked back down at me. "I don't know," he said.

"Should we try and do the A-frame thing again? Or do a different position?"

Simon raised his eyebrows at me, giving me a crooked grin. "A different position, huh?"

I felt my cheeks grow warm, but couldn't help smiling. "You…behave yourself," I said.

"A-frame again," Simon said. "Ready?" I nodded, getting my footing steady beneath me. Simon let go of the rope and held his hand out. "When you're ready, take my hand."

I nodded again. I let go of the rope and was about to

press my palm to Simon's when Ducky yelled my name from the other platform.

It was just enough of a distraction. My hand slipped past Simon's and I fell forward into him, and then both of us were falling, falling, the air flying past us, our limbs tangled. I'm pretty sure I screamed. The harness tightened around my thighs and hips, and then Simon and I were in a heap on the ground.

Simon scrambled to his feet, then lifted me onto mine, holding my shoulders and gazing into my face. "Are you okay?" he said. "Marlowe?"

"Fucking hell!" I yelled. Then I flung myself into his arms, clinging to him. Adrenaline coursed through my body, and I was having a hard time convincing myself that I was safe on solid ground. It's like all of the terror I had felt from falling was still coursing through me. I was vaguely aware of a string of nonsense coming out of my mouth. "Why did…that was…too tall from the ground… Jesus Christ…that…"

"Hey," Simon said. "It's okay," he whispered. "I've got you. I've got you. I've got you."

And it was this tender repetition that finally allowed me to calm down. Once my heart rate was closer to normal, I felt like an idiot. Of course we were fine. I pulled away from Simon and punched him in the arm. "What kind of pirate are you!?" I exclaimed.

Simon didn't answer. He just smiled and held out his hand. "Come on," he said.

CHAPTER 18

Wanna Go Somewhere?

JULY 24: PORTLAND, OREGON

SIMON

I intentionally spent the whole day with Aaron yesterday. Because I still didn't know how to talk to Marlowe about our kiss. Or our uh…moment in the van. Or the ropes course, or any of it. We played a show the night of the ropes course, and it was great, and we played another show last night and it was great, too. And we still hadn't talked. But today we all had the whole day free, and I wasn't sure how much longer I could avoid the subject.

I stayed in bed until noon, trying to make a plan. I finally had the idea of a walk, so I made my way upstairs before I could talk myself out of it. I found Marlowe in the dining room, scrolling her phone while eating a bowl of cereal.

Why did she look so pretty *all* the time? Even now, with her dark hair in a messy bun on the top of her head, and no makeup, and wearing a faded t-shirt and shorts. I wanted to kiss her *all the time*.

"Morning," I said. She looked up at me, and the sight

of her blue eyes filled my whole chest with something light and fluttery.

"Morning," she replied.

"I uh…I'm going…wanna go on a weird walk with me today?"

I cringed internally. I sounded like I was asking a girl to the prom or something.

Marlowe looked at me for a moment and then smiled. "Hell yeah, brother," she said.

When she smiled at me like that, I couldn't help but smile back. "Meet you in an hour?"

As soon as I started to get ready, I realized I hadn't actually made a plan of what to say on this walk. I spent the next hour torturing myself over it. Because I wanted to respect whatever she wanted. And I totally understood why the Oregon Rule existed. But I also wanted…her. The hunger I felt for Marlowe, for every part of her—her body and her eyes and her laughter, was only increasing. Our kiss a few days ago didn't satisfy that hunger at all. It just made it worse. I wanted to be with Marlowe all the time, in every sense.

But I also didn't want to make any decisions on my own.

By pure chance, Marlowe and I opened our bedroom doors at the exact same time. She stood in her doorway, her dark hair falling in gentle waves around her face, wearing some sort of romper and combat boots, looking like the girl of my dreams.

"Hey," she said.

"Hey."

"There's a park nearby," she said. "I thought we could start there."

I nodded. We went upstairs, told the others we were going on a walk, and then headed outside and down the driveway. It took everything in me to not grasp Marlowe's hand.

The park was only a few blocks away, and there wasn't anything weird in front of any of the houses we passed. Which was a good thing, actually, because I needed to bring up…us, before a weird sighting ended the walk.

The park was huge, with a playground and a dog run and tons of trees. Because it was the middle of summer, it was filled with people. We'd just barely walked past the gates of the park when Marlowe pointed.

"Look!" she cried.

I followed her finger to an ice cream stand, then frowned. "That's not weird," I said.

"No, I know," Marlowe said. "I just want ice cream."

"Oh," I laughed. "Then let's get ice cream."

Ten minutes later, we were sitting on a park bench, vanilla soft serve cones in our hands. "This was the right choice," Marlowe said.

I watched her tongue swipe over her ice cream and immediately had to look away. The way the sight had turned me on made me feel slightly insane.

"Does it count if you see something weird while not walking?" I asked.

"Why, do you see something?"

"No, just…hypothetically." I caught a drip of my rapidly melting ice cream cone, then heard Marlowe laughing. I turned to her. "What?" I asked.

"The truly weird thing is how messily you are eating that ice cream right now," Marlowe said.

"Huh?"

"You have ice cream all over your hand. And face."

I glanced down at my hand, and Marlowe was right. "I'm doing the best I can, here," I said.

"Here," she said. "You've got…"

Marlowe reached out and ran a finger over a spot near the corner of my mouth.

Electricity rushed through me at her touch. I watched her eyes as they lingered on my mouth. For a brief second, every possibility hung in the air between us. And then she leaned in and kissed me.

I dropped my ice cream cone and took her face in my hands, kissing her back. She tasted like vanilla and summer and every perfect thing I'd ever wanted. She let out a whimper and it took every ounce of my self-control to stop from pushing her down on that park bench and covering her body with mine.

After what was either five seconds or five minutes, Marlowe pulled away. My lips chased after hers for a half second before I opened my eyes to find her smiling at me.

"Simon?" she said, sounding breathless.

"Yeah?" I asked, my chest heaving just as much as hers was.

"This is great but you have ice cream all over your hands and it's kind of getting all over me." Marlowe's eyes were dancing with laughter, and I noticed the sticky smears I had left on her cheeks and jawline.

I laughed. "Sorry," I said. "Wait, hang on." I walked over to the ice cream stand and got a handful of napkins, then ran some of them under a drinking fountain. I brought them back to Marlowe on the park bench, where both of us cleaned ourselves up, sitting side by side.

"What happened to your ice cream?" she asked.

I glanced around, then pointed to it on the sidewalk, where the remains of my ice cream cone sat melting. Then I leaned in and pressed my lips to hers again. I could feel her smile beneath my kiss. "Worth it," I whispered.

I pulled away in time to see Marlowe toss her own ice cream cone over her shoulder, then lunge for me. Our kisses started with laughter, but within seconds, heat was building between us. I tangled my hand into Marlowe's hair, trying to pull her closer to me, my tongue seeking hers.

"Simon," she gasped between kisses.

"Marlowe," I whispered back. Hearing me say her name did something to her, and with a tiny moan, Marlowe pressed herself closer to me. One of her legs was half flung over mine, and I was realizing how inconvenient it was to make out while sitting side by side on a hard park bench like this. One of my hands crept between our bodies up her ribs, my fingers barely brushing the bottom of her tits. I wanted desperately to reach farther up, cup her breast, fill my hands with her, but there was still one small part of my mind that was aware that we were in public.

"Simon, what are…what are we doing?"

I pressed kisses along the side of her neck. I knew this was the conversation we were supposed to be having, the entire reason I suggested a walk. But I couldn't concentrate when she smelled so good and when her skin was warm and soft and when she let out those little noises. "I don't know," I said. "But can we keep doing it?"

Marlowe pulled me up to face her, her blue eyes looked steadily at me. "What about the rules?"

I pressed my forehead against hers and spoke without thinking. "Maybe some rules are worth breaking," I whispered. As soon as I said it, I knew it was true. We could figure out the rest later. Right now I just wanted to be with Marlowe. I buried my face in her neck again, licking at her skin.

I heard her breath quicken. "Do you wanna go somewhere?"

"Where," I murmured, not willing to draw my lips away.

"Anywhere," Marlowe said, her voice straining. "Somewhere with a bed."

I managed to raise my head enough to look at her. Her pupils were wide, her cheeks flushed. I swallowed. "How do you feel about shitty motels?" I asked.

Marlowe nodded. "Please just take me somewhere with a bed."

"Bed, got it," I said. "Just…um…give me a minute."

"No, now!" Marlowe said, looking desperate. "Why?"

I looked at her and lowered my voice. "Because I have a raging boner right now and I don't want to walk through a public park like this."

Marlowe's look grew heated, and she gazed down at my lap, where I was trying to use one hand to keep my arousal hidden without being too obvious. She laid a hand on my thigh and looked back at my face, biting her lip. She looked as lustful as I felt.

"That's…not helping," I said, my voice sounding slightly strangled.

Marlowe stood. "Find a place and text me the address," she said. "I'll meet you there."

She turned and sauntered away, and I watched her shapely legs for a full thirty seconds before pulling out my phone and googling motels near me.

Planet Motel

JULY 24: PORTLAND, OREGON

MARLOWE

I walked straight to the nearest CVS and grabbed a 10-pack box of condoms. I kept checking my phone, waiting for Simon to text me an address. Or to text me "never mind, this is a bad idea." Which I really really hoped he would not do.

Because right at this moment, I did not care if it was a bad or a good idea. I wanted him so much I could barely walk in a straight line.

As I walked out of the drugstore, my phone dinged with an address two blocks away. I practically ran to the "Planet Motel."

If I wasn't so crazed with lust, I would have stopped to appreciate the 1960s space theme of the motel. I would have taken a picture of the spinning sign out front, a friendly-looking alien waving from a flying saucer. A sight weird enough to end a weird walk. But all I could think about was Simon, so I marched straight over to room 109 and raised my hand to knock.

He flung the door open and for a second, we just stood there, looking at each other. I took in his brown curls, his intense green eyes, the way his T-shirt stretched across his chest. Images flashed through my mind of him onstage, giving audiences that crooked smile, his fingers moving over the frets of his guitar, his jaw tensing as he sang into the mic. And now he was here, standing in front of me, alone in this motel doorway.

We both stepped forward at the same time, our lips crashing against each other's. Simon pulled me into the room, and I fumbled to close the door behind us. I couldn't figure out which part of him to touch first—I ran my hands down his arms, through his hair, across his chest. When my fingertips got to the hem of his shirt, brushing against his warm skin, he let out a groan before reaching up and yanking his shirt over his head. He braced his arms on either side of me.

I spread my palms over his stomach, feeling the hard lines of muscle flexing there. I looked up at him with wide eyes. "Simon…" I managed.

I needed more of him. I reached up to pull down the zipper of my romper, shoving it down my legs. I made quick work of my bra and then pulled Simon back toward me, our bodies flush, skin to skin.

Maybe it was too fast, but I couldn't bring myself to slow down.

His kisses were sending me to dizzying heights, and I could feel my nipples hardening against his chest. I started to push him toward the bed, but quickly realized that my romper was still around my ankles, stuck on my boots. I let out a giggle.

"What?" Simon asked, breaking away to look at me.

"My shoes are still on," I said. "I wanted to move us to the bed, but this whole situation is a tripping hazard."

Simon dropped to his knees in front of me. He unlaced my boots, then yanked them off. He pulled my romper off my ankles, then my socks, then looked up at me. I stood there, in nothing but my yellow underwear, gazing at this man kneeling in front of me. Simon's face was even with my belly button. I reached down to run my hands through his hair. He looked at me, then turned his attention to my stomach. His hands gripped the sides of my thighs and then slid up, brushing over my hips, covering my ribs. Finally, his palms moved over my breasts, and I arched into his touch.

He massaged me, his thumbs brushing over my nipples, filling my whole body with sensation. I felt his warm lips against my stomach, and reached back to brace myself against the wall. Simon looked up at me again, his hair falling into his eyes a little. He kissed a little lower, moving closer to where I wanted him, his eyes still on my face.

I squirmed against the wall, trying to resist the urge to lift a leg over Simon's shoulder, to grab his head and bury it between my legs.

He teased me with his hot breath, his lips skating over me, closer and closer to my clit. My knees were actually trembling by that point.

"Simon, I'm not going to…we gotta…I can't stand up when you're…"

He stood, grinning at me, then dragged me farther into the room. I fell backward onto the bed, then watched as Simon crawled up my body. He dragged a hand down from my throat, between my breasts, to land at the fabric of my panties.

"Can I take these off?" he asked.

I nodded so vigorously that it affected my vision. "Take your pants off, too. Please."

Simon grinned. "Only because you said please."

He stood and unzipped his pants, pulling them down, kicking off his shoes while he was at it. I thought of how I had listened to him do this same thing—take his pants off—back in Crescent City, the way just the *sound* of it turned me on. I loved getting to watch him now. Simon's cock was hard in his boxers, and at the sight of it, I felt a rush of heat between my legs.

He knelt on the bed next to me, then hooked his fingers into my panties, pulling them slowly down my legs. At the sight of my naked body in front of him, he made a hungry kind of sound in his throat.

"Fuck, you're gorgeous," he said.

"Come here," I replied. I pulled him on top of me, letting him settle his weight between my legs. He leaned down to kiss me, our tongues tangling. After a while, I felt Simon's hips grind up into me, the hardness of him rubbing right on my most sensitive spot through his boxers. I let out another moan.

"Condoms," I gasped.

"What?" Simon said, his voice breathless. He tilted his hips into me again. And then again.

"I bought…condoms," I managed. "By the door."

Simon pushed himself up and hovered above me. His chest was heaving, and already sweat was making the hairs on his forehead curl slightly. "I bought some, too," he grinned. "A ten pack."

"So we have…" Another grind of his hips, another moan. "…at least twenty times…" I shut my eyes, the hard length of this man between my legs making me gasp and whimper. "…to do this."

Simon stilled, and I opened my eyes to look at him. "Marlowe, I'm going to be honest," he said. I froze. Did he not want to do this?

"I um…I might not last very long inside of you," he

finished. My entire body filled with fire. The idea that I was so attractive to him that he didn't think he could last long was so hot I could hardly think straight. Then I saw the determined glint in his eye. "So I'm going to do everything I can to make you come before that happens."

I didn't think my heart could be pounding any harder, but then Simon reached down between our bodies and slid his fingers over me, and I genuinely thought I might die of pleasure. My eyes fluttered shut.

"Is that good?" Simon whispered, his voice low and husky, and I swear that alone almost sent me over the edge.

I nodded. "Faster," I whispered. Simon's movements quickened and he leaned down to kiss that sensitive spot on the side of my neck.

"Fuck, Simon," I gritted out. I clutched at his shoulders, trying to stifle the desperate noises his touch was bringing out in me.

I felt his lips brush my ear. "There's no one staying in the rooms next to us," he whispered. "You can be as loud as you want, sweetheart."

The sound I made then was practically pornographic. My hips were writhing, chasing the ecstasy Simon was giving me.

"Goddamn, you're so beautiful," Simon said, his voice sounding strained. I opened my eyes to see him looking down at me, his fingers still working fast between my legs. Tension was building inside of me, climbing higher and higher.

Simon's chest rose and fell as he worked. "I want to watch you come," he breathed. His voice dipped into a low murmur, and his lips brushed my ear. "Is this enough for you? Will my fingers bring you there? Marlowe, tell me how to make you come."

But I didn't need to tell him. Two more seconds of his

touch and my climax tore through me, causing my back to lift off the bed, my moans echoing off the walls. I was vaguely aware of shouting Simon's name at some point. Simon didn't stop moving his fingers until I was collapsed and languid with pleasure, my chest heaving.

"Holy shit," Simon said. "That was the hottest thing I've ever seen in my life."

CHAPTER 20
Since April

JULY 24: PORTLAND, OREGON

SIMON

I stared down at Marlowe, her body slick with sweat, still trembling from her climax. This perfect, beautiful girl was naked in bed in front of me, her breathing slowly coming back down to normal after the orgasm that I gave her.

I could die happy right now.

Or. Almost. My cock twitched in my boxers. Marlowe opened her eyes and looked up at me.

"Kiss me," she whispered.

I braced my hands on either side of her head and leaned down to press my lips to hers. She moaned into my mouth, her legs widening and then wrapping around me. I ground into her, my body seeking the heat of her.

Then I felt her hands press hard against my chest and I froze. I lifted myself up to look at her. "Is this okay?" I asked.

"Yes, go get a condom," Marlowe replied, her face flushed, her voice breathless.

I practically leapt from the bed, shoving my boxers down to my ankles. I ripped open the box of condoms I'd bought, and I had never noticed how many fucking steps there were to putting on a condom before now. I was going to die.

Finally, I knelt in front of Marlowe again. She let her knees fall open, and I laid my body over hers. After a deep breath, I pushed myself inside of her.

We both moaned. My head dropped to her shoulder as I began to move. She was perfect. Everything about Marlowe was perfect. Her full lips, her strong legs, the tightness of her body around me.

I started to thrust faster, and as I did, Marlowe's cries grew higher and higher in pitch, her body tensing.

"Again?" I managed to ask her.

She just nodded, her brow furrowed in pleasure, her mouth open. Goddamn, I had to last just a little longer for her. I pulled out and flipped her body around so that she was on all fours.

"Hold on to the bed frame," I gritted out.

Marlowe reached up to brace herself, and after I pushed myself inside of her, I brought a hand around to squeeze one of her tits. My hips were already moving sloppily, but I used my other hand to brush my thumb over her clit and somehow, by the grace of god, managed to control myself long enough to feel her throbbing around me, crying out as another climax caused her to grip the bed frame so hard her knuckles were white.

While she was still shuddering, I thrust up into her, fast, desperate, for only a few more moments, until my own release came roaring through me. When it was over, we both collapsed onto the bed, feeling the last pulses of our climaxes fade into perfect satisfaction.

"Fuck," I breathed.

Marlowe turned to smile at me. Her hair was tangled, her lips were red and swollen, and a thin layer of sweat made her skin glow.

"Fuck," she agreed.

I couldn't even form coherent thoughts for a good few minutes…I just laid there staring at the ceiling. When I could function again, I turned to Marlowe.

"You have no idea how long I've wanted to do that," I said.

She turned her blue eyes to me. "Probably about as long as I've wanted to do that."

I grinned, then turned my body so that I could kiss her, slow and tender this time. Then I looked up, and for the first time since getting here, I actually took in the decor of the room.

I was pretty sure the carpet hadn't been changed since 1962. Or the wallpaper, which had metallic accents to it. Framed photos of alien invasion headlines hung on the walls.

"We keep sharing beds in super tacky places," I said.

Marlowe glanced around, then sat up. "Whoa." Then she turned back to me with a grin. "This time was way more fun."

"I dunno, you wearing my boxers was pretty hot."

Marlowe gripped my arm. "Oh my god I know I was dying!!!"

We laughed and kissed again.

"I'm going to clean up," I said. "Do you need anything?"

"Just…hurry back."

When I was done, I returned to the bed and pulled Marlowe onto my chest.

"How long do you have the motel for?" Marlowe asked, her fingers tracing shapes down my torso.

"Technically until tomorrow morning," I replied. "Although, uh…we probably shouldn't stay away that long."

Marlowe's hand stilled. "Yeah," she said. Both of us were silent for a few moments. "The Oregon Rule is all kinds of broken," she finally said.

I looked down at her. "Do you regret it?"

Marlowe turned her face up to look at me. "No," she said. "Do you?"

I shook my head. "I've been thinking about this since April."

At that, Marlowe rolled so that she was half on top of me and started covering my face and neck and chest with kisses. I chuckled, reaching up to touch her hair. "Same," she whispered between kisses.

Marlowe was slowly trailing kisses down my stomach, and apparently I had a very short refractory period with her because I was already getting hard again. Which meant I really had to say something before I was unable to think.

"Marlowe?" I said. But then she wrapped her lips around my cock, and I groaned.

"Hmmm?" she asked, humming while I was in her mouth, and the sensation caused my eyes to roll back in my head.

"Marlowe…unhh…wait, sweetheart…Marlowe, wait."

She released me and lifted her eyes to mine, and I didn't think I'd ever seen anything more gorgeous in my life. Her lips full and wet, her dark hair in tangled waves around her face, her naked body.

I closed my eyes so that I could form a coherent sentence. "What are we going to do?"

Her hand wrapped around my dick. "I hope that's obvious," she said, and I could hear her grin in her voice.

But I opened my eyes and put my hands on her shoulders.

"Before we do this again—which I'm super willing to do, by the way—I think we should…talk. About this. Us. The Oregon Rule. All of it."

Marlowe removed her hand, which I hated, but it also allowed me to concentrate a little better. "What do *you* think we should do?" she asked.

I swallowed. "Well, the rule's already broken. But I think…telling everyone would cause more problems." Marlowe nodded, and I took a deep breath. "I think we're mature enough to deal with, I dunno, anything that happens between us. So I say we tell people after the tour?"

"Tell people we broke the rule or that we're into each other?"

Marlowe saying out loud that she was into me was almost too much to process. But I was so clearly into her that I figured I might as well say it out loud, too. I swallowed again. "Tell people that we're into each other."

"What about after the tour? Aren't you guys playing somewhere else?"

I nodded. "Colorado. But only for two weeks."

Marlowe moved one of her legs so that she was straddling my thighs. Then she reached down to my dick again. "And we can keep doing this?" She pumped me slowly once, twice. My head fell back and hit the headboard.

"God, yes," I replied.

"Right now and during the rest of the tour and after the tour?"

"Yes."

And then Marlowe worked me with her hands and mouth until I thought I was going to explode, and then rolled another condom on before sinking down onto me. It was slower this time, less desperate, her hips rolling lazily until they weren't anymore and both of us were crying out.

I didn't know when we'd have another opportunity to share a bed on tour, so we took advantage of it two more times before leaving.

~

WE HELD hands on the walk back to the Airbnb. About a block away, Marlowe stopped us. "What are we going to say?" she asked.

I glanced at the time on my phone and thought for a moment. "That we went on a weird walk and then went to a movie?"

"What movie?"

"I dunno, pick one."

She punched me gently in the arm. "We should have a good story," she said. "What if they ask us about the movie?"

"Fine, we were on a weird walk in the park and then someone approached us with a flyer to invite us to their surrealist indie film about immigration reform so we went to that at a local bar and that counted as the weird thing that ended our walk."

Marlowe stared at me. "Did you just come up with that right now?" I nodded. "Damn," she said, smiling at me.

That smile was going to be the death of me. I had no idea how I was going to keep this a secret. I was so incredibly into her that I was sure it would be obvious. It probably had been for a while. How was I going to survive hanging out in the greenroom, eating dinners together, sleeping in the same place? All I wanted to do all the time now was kiss her. And hold her hand. And hold her…all of her. I sighed. We only had a week and a half left of the tour. We just had to make it until then.

CHAPTER 21

It's About You

MARLOWE

If ever there was a doubt in my mind that I had a big ole crush on Simon Burroughs, it was long gone. I'd spent the last 24 hours reliving every second in that motel room. Now we were at sound check and Simon was currently tuning his guitar and I was trying really hard to fight off the erotic thoughts I was having about his fingers.

Ducky walked up, carrying her snare drum case. "Dude, have you guys seen that alien motel a few blocks from our Airbnb? I never noticed it until today and it's incredible!"

Simon and I locked eyes, and I tried to hide my grin.

"Yeah, we saw it on our weird walk yesterday," Simon said. Which was technically true, and him saying it so smoothly made me want to unbuckle his belt. I reminded myself of the Oregon Rule out of habit. But then I remembered that we had already broken the Oregon Rule, so I had to remind myself of the new rule: to keep it all under wraps. Protect your band mates and the tour. I needed to come up with some catchy name. The "Boy Scout Rule"? The Boy Scout Rule. Don't tell. Scout's honor.

Felix's voice interrupted my thoughts. "Queen Anne, come sound check for the tree song."

I dared to exchange a smile with Simon, and then headed onto the stage.

THE AUDIENCE HAD LOVED US, and now they were screaming their brains out for the Boy Scouts of Atlantis. They were playing the sexy siren song again, and I was having a real hard time keeping my thoughts G-rated. They had played it at every show since that first one, but tonight was different. The words took on a new meaning now that I knew what Simon looked like without his clothes on. Now that I knew the way his neck muscles tightened when he came. Now that I knew the sounds he made, the way his lips moved when he kissed.

On the chorus, Simon looked down at me in the audience and I could not tear my eyes away. He sang those words directly to me, my pussy ringing like a bell.

Breaking me down
Breaking me up
Breaking me down
Breaking me up
I give up I give in
She can be my sin
The temptation is cruel
I will break all the rules
For her

I never wanted this tour to end, so that I could hang out with Simon all the time. And also, the tour really needed to end so that when he sang this song, I could climb onto the stage and kiss the hell out of him.

At the end of the song, Simon looked at me and grinned, his brown curls falling into his eyes. Then he turned back to the audience.

"Thanks everyone! Now we want to invite Queen Anne back onstage with us." He reached out his hand, and I took it to let him pull me up.

He brought his lips to the microphone again, while all of us took our places. "We all wrote this when we were in the Redwoods in California. I don't know if any of you have been out there, but those are some big fucking trees. We all camped out there and wrote this song, and the chorus is really simple, so sing along when you know it."

I would never get over how *into* the tree song the audiences were. We'd basically added it to every set we played since Corvallis, and every time, the whole venue was singing along by the second chorus. It had grown from a folksy acoustic jam into a rock jam and it was a blast every single time.

And bonus, I liked sharing a mic with Simon. Sure, the venue might have had another mic for me, but I didn't want to give up the opportunity to have my lips close to that guy's. When we weren't grinning at the audience, we grinned at each other.

SINCE IT WAS our last night in Portland, we'd decided on a group dinner. But then we couldn't decide what to eat, so eventually we all ordered Taco Bell and ate it around the table in the Airbnb. Now everyone was sitting around the living room in their pajamas and talking. I watched Simon step outside onto the back porch, and after a few minutes, I followed.

I stepped through the back door to find Simon leaning on the porch railing. He was wearing pajama pants and a t-shirt, his hair damp from a shower. I wanted desperately to wrap my arms around him, but couldn't figure out how to do it without looking suspicious as hell. So instead, I came and stood next to him, not quite close enough to touch.

"Hey," I said.

He turned and smiled at me. "Hey," he replied.

I gazed up at the sky. There weren't many stars visible, but I could hear crickets in the grass, and the wooden planks of the patio were warm beneath my bare feet. I loved summer nights more than I could express. I closed my eyes for a moment, just taking it all in. Finally I turned back to Simon. He was staring out into the yard. I could see a glimpse of his tattoo, peeking out from under his sleeve, and I smiled.

"Cool tattoo," I said.

He turned to me. "Thanks," he said, his eyes dancing. "This really pretty girl talked me into getting it."

Butterflies exploded in my chest, and I held in a giggle. I never thought of myself as much of a giggler but apparently Simon did something to me. I liked being called pretty. I liked it when *he* said I was pretty.

"It looks really good on your arm," I said. I reached out to grasp his bicep. "You've got good arms for tattoos."

"I've got good arms for a lot of things," Simon replied. His voice was low and suggestive, and I felt a rush of heat move through me, a pinch in my nipples. I could still hear the others talking inside, just a few feet away. Simon and I had better pump the brakes on this flirting or else I was going to do something to make it real obvious something was going on between us.

I let go of his arm and leaned on the railing. "That was a good show tonight," I said.

Simon grinned. "That trees song goes hard."

"It's because it's so sing-along-able," I said. "Audiences really get into it." I paused, thinking about the Boy Scouts' set. "That siren song," I said. I dared to look over at him. "The new one? I don't think I've told you yet how hot that song is."

In the darkness, I saw Simon's ears turn pink. "It's uh…thanks."

"You're a fucking good songwriter," I said.

Simon turned to me, searching my face, seeming to debate something with himself. Finally, he turned back to look into the yard. His voice was a whisper when he spoke. "It's about you."

My mouth fell open. "It's…what?"

He turned to look at me again, his eyes heated, his voice still low. "I was trying to…I dunno, when I wrote it, I was trying to put everything I was feeling into a song so that maybe I could like, function? Like the song could contain all my…want, or whatever."

I was having trouble breathing. And keeping my hands to myself. "I think I wanted it to be about me," I managed. And it was true. "I don't think I fully realized it until right this second, but holy shit. This is the hottest thing that has ever happened to me."

"You're the hottest thing that's ever happened to me." Simon turned and leaned his hip against the railing, smiling at me.

I stared at him. "I want to kiss you so bad right now," I whispered.

Simon glanced toward the house, then quickly leaned down and pressed his lips to my cheek. "You'll just have to think about it," he whispered.

Then he walked inside, leaving me a puddle in the summer night.

CHAPTER 22

Meet Me In the Bathroom

JULY 29: ASHLAND, OREGON

SIMON

If anyone were to ask me what Eugene, Oregon was like, I'd have to reply, "I have no idea, because the only thing I could pay attention to was Marlowe." We played two shows there, and my main memories of them are of singing "Siren" directly to Marlowe while trying to pretend I wasn't, and managing to sneak away to make out with her for a few minutes while everyone was packing up.

Now we were sound checking in Ashland, Oregon, and I was pretty sure my crush on her was reaching some kind of critical mass. We just had to make it to August 5. That was only a week. And then we could stop sneaking around and start making up for lost time. (Making out for lost time?)

I was trying not to watch Marlowe tune her guitar at sound check, when four people I didn't recognize walked in—three boys and one girl, all of them carrying instruments.

"Hey all!" one of the guys called out.

Jem looked up. "Are you guys 'Voluntary Commitment'?"

"That's us!" the girl replied. She set a guitar case down. "I'm Brooklyn."

Oh, yeah. I'd been so preoccupied with Marlowe that I'd forgotten we were being joined by another band for the next few shows. They were playing with us here in Ashland and then again in Redding. We were going to be splitting an Airbnb with them in a few days.

The rest of the band members introduced themselves —Tate, Colton, and Evan—and the Boy Scouts and Queen Anne all said our names. I felt an unfamiliar resentment bubble up as I watched everyone chat. We'd created a little tour family, the eight of us, playing all over the west coast, and I didn't want anyone coming in to mess it up.

Someone bumped my shoulder, and I turned to see Aaron standing next to me. "Grumpy?" he asked quietly.

Shit. My thoughts must have been more visible on my face than I thought. I shook my head. "Just…trying to remember everyone's names," I lied.

BUT A FEW HOURS LATER, when Voluntary Commitment got onstage, my annoyance with them was replaced with pure, insane musical appreciation. They were so fucking good. They had such a *tight* sound—their drummer was a human metronome, and everyone was locked in to that rhythm, and the singer, Tate, was the kind of performer that made me wonder if I'd ever actually done a good show in my life. I'm sure a lesser man would have been jealous, but I was just too impressed to feel anything else.

Thank god we went on first. The Boy Scouts did a short-ish set, then Queen Anne, and we skipped our tree song finale to leave time for the new band.

In the middle of one of their songs, the guitarist, Brooklyn, came up to the front of the stage to solo, and next to me, Aaron screamed and then pretended to faint against me. When I got him back to his feet, he screamed some more, and then turned to me.

"I think I'm in love!" he shouted. I grinned at him.

Marlowe was standing on my other side, moving her body in time with the music, her eyes closed, her head thrown back.

There is a Venn diagram of "experiencing a good rock show" and "having good sex" and they are *not* two separate circles. A good guitar chord can literally turn someone on. (Someone like me. To be specific.) Right now, listening to the music, watching Marlowe move to it, I was hovering in the overlap between those circles.

Marlowe was wearing a tank top and a short, fluffy tutu, and I wanted to run my hands down her arms and let her dance against me.

"Goddamn Oregon Rule," Aaron said.

I whipped my head over to look at him, but he was staring up at Brooklyn onstage.

Right.

The song built to a crescendo and then ended, and the whole venue erupted. Aaron jumped up and down, and I could see the rest of my tour mates doing the same thing.

Except Marlowe. Marlowe had turned to me, a heated look on her face. She put a hand on my arm and stood on my tiptoes to speak into my ear.

"Meet me in the bathroom in one minute," she said. Then she turned and walked away.

Voluntary Commitment started in to their next song,

and I felt it in my bones. In the back of my mind, some small voice was shouting *What the hell are you doing!? This is so fucking risky!* But I couldn't bring myself to listen. There is only one thing I will leave a good rock show for.

I stood and fidgeted for what I guessed was one minute before making my way to the back of the venue.

When I got to the back of the venue, I froze. There were four bathrooms, all of them single use. But I had no idea which one Marlowe was in. I stared for a few seconds, but then one of the doors cracked open and Marlowe glanced out. After looking around quickly to make sure no one was paying attention, I followed her inside.

As soon as the door was shut, she shoved me against it. Her mouth slotted over mine and my arms tightened around her body. It was like we were both starving, and didn't know when our next meal would be.

I flipped us so that her back was against the door and slotted one of my legs between hers. She let out a stifled moan and I brought my hands to her tits.

"You feel so fucking good," I managed between kisses. The music thudded in the room outside, and I felt Marlowe rolling her hips in time to it. I smiled into her mouth, then brought one of my hands down between her legs.

Or I tried to. I was met with roughly five yards of fabric. Miles of fabric? All I knew was that there was way too much clothing between my hands and Marlowe's body. I fumbled for a few minutes before muttering, "The fuck? How many layers do you have on?"

Marlowe laughed and gathered her petticoats up to her waist, then shoved her fishnets and panties down. She grabbed my wrist and brought my fingers right to where both of us wanted them. We groaned in unison.

"You're so goddamn wet," I whispered, my fingers slick with her arousal.

Her hand found my cock, rubbing me over my clothes, and I leaned down to kiss her again. We were both moving against each other, hands and lips and bodies in rhythm, and it was perfect, and—

Knock knock knock.

Both Marlowe and I froze. She looked up at me with wide eyes. Then she brought a hand to her mouth to stifle a giggle.

Knock knock knock.

"Just a minute!" I called out. Then I mouthed, "What do we do?"

Marlowe yanked her clothes back into place and searched my face. I could actually see the moment the idea came into her mind. She reached into my pocket to grab my phone, which was…very distracting. But then she lifted it and snapped a picture of a doodle someone had made on the wall, then handed my phone back to me. Before I could figure out what she was doing, she flung the door open.

Rose stood in front of us. Her eyebrows flew up when she saw both of us in the bathroom together.

Fuck.

But Marlowe just smiled. "I had to show him some bathroom art for his Instagram."

I swallowed, then held up my phone as proof.

Rose frowned at us, but didn't say anything as we stepped around her to let her inside. Marlowe casually made her way back to the stage. I decided to stay in the shadows for a few more minutes, until my cock had calmed down enough for me to join the crowd.

That was fucking close. Seeing Rose's face just now…I

didn't like that we were deceiving her. A twinge of guilt twisted in my stomach. But then I thought of Marlowe's hands and lips on me, and I couldn't think about anything else.

Damn, I liked her.

CHAPTER 23

Seeing Other People

JULY 30: REDDING, CALIFORNIA

MARLOWE

On the drive to Redding, Ducky and I were busy scream-singing along to her road trip playlist when my phone buzzed in my pocket.

I tried to hide my grin when I saw Simon's name on the screen, and tilted my phone away from Ducky's view.

> SIMON: Hey so that was a close call last night

> SIMON: In the bathroom

> SIMON: With Rose

I sighed. I knew he was right. Maybe we were playing a little fast and loose with the Oregon Rule. Or our complete disregard for it.

ME: Yeah. I don't think she suspects anything tho? If she does, she didn't say anything to me

SIMON: Let's go on a weird walk and talk about it when we get to Redding

I kind of didn't want to talk about it but I did want to go on a weird walk with Simon, mostly because it meant we could probably find somewhere to fool around for a while. But he was probably right.

As soon as we unloaded gear and luggage and picked rooms at the Airbnb, Simon and I headed out.

As soon as we were out of sight, Simon took my hand and yanked me to him. One of his hands held the back of my head, keeping me in place so he could lean down and kiss me.

I didn't think I would ever get tired of kissing Simon Burroughs.

By the time we stopped, we were both out of breath. We stood looking at each other.

"Goddamn," I said.

"Yeah." Simon turned and started walking, one of my hands in his. "So I have an idea, and I kind of hate it, and you might hate it too, but I think it might be a good idea."

"What is it?"

"We…see other people?"

I froze. "We what?"

"Not seriously!" Simon explained. He looked at me with worried eyes. "That came out wrong. Just…like, tonight, at the show. Flirt with someone else. An audience member."

I resumed walking. "Throw 'em off the track, huh?"

"Yeah," Simon said. "And also…"

My stomach filled with dread. "And also?"

"I don't know. It might be a good idea in general. Just to make sure things stay casual between us until we get home next week."

I was immediately flooded with anxiety. Was Simon trying to pump the brakes because he didn't like me as much as I liked him? Maybe this really was casual for him. But he said "casual until next week," so maybe he was just truly trying to keep us from becoming too obvious.

I frowned. "You're right, I do hate that."

"I know," Simon said, looking apologetic.

"But maybe you're right," I sighed. "I don't know." I stole a glance at him. "What if I flirt with a stranger but I'm still into you on the inside?"

Simon grinned at me. How was he so goddamn handsome? "That works for me."

"Deal," I said. "So should we actually look for something weird on this walk or do you wanna find someplace where we can feel each other up?"

Simon glanced around the neighborhood we were currently walking in. "I don't know if we can find someplace private enough to actually feel each other up, but we can definitely keep kissing."

I smiled at him. I was so so so so happy. Having Simon's hand in mine. Knowing he wanted to kiss me as much as I wanted to kiss him. God, I couldn't wait until we got back to Alameda.

"Then let's keep walking and kissing," I said.

Voluntary Commitment's set was...weirdly strained that night. They played first and everything sounded great, but there wasn't quite the same level of joyful banter onstage. It just wasn't as obvious how much they loved the music—you couldn't feel it tonight the way we could the last show. They just seemed tense.

Or maybe it was just me that was tense. Simon and I agreed to not stand next to each other when Voluntary Commitment was playing, and I was scanning the crowd to find a stranger to flirt with.

And apparently my heterosexuality had morphed into Simonsexuality because literally no one looked attractive to me but him.

I had it bad.

I glanced around the room, taking note of everyone who looked close enough to my age to flirt with. The inventory was looking…bleak.

Guy at the bar with a backwards hat and a flannel shirt. A beer in each hand. Maybe? I watched as he snorted and then spit on the ground near his feet.

Nope.

There was a dude bobbing his head to the music in one of the booths. Impressive beard. Cool piercings. Maybe? I took a step toward him just as a stunning redhead slid into the seat next to him and kissed his cheek.

Nope again.

I continued my scan of the room. A burly man stood near the back door, dressed all in black, trying to hide the fact that he was vaping. There was rebelliousness about that that I appreciated. I stared at the ground for a moment, contemplating. I didn't often just approach strangers. How did people do this? What line could I even use? Call him on his secret vaping maybe? Yeah, that could work.

I looked up and the man was gone. I sighed. When he came back, maybe I'd make a move. I glanced around the room to look for Simon. I really didn't want to watch him flirt with someone else. Even if I knew it was fake. But when I found him, he was making his way backstage. The Boy Scouts of Atlantis were up next.

I spent the next fifteen minutes trying to work up the courage (or enthusiasm) to talk to the guy in black. I had just about made up my mind to go for it when the Boy Scouts played the opening chords of "Siren."

I looked up at Simon on the stage. His tight black pants and graphic tee. The forest green button-up he had open, the sleeves rolled up to his elbows. I watched his brown curls move to the music as he played, his jaw tight with concentration. I looked at his fingers moving over the frets of his guitar and I had one thought.

I might be in love with Simon Burroughs.

The thought made my blood rush. *I might actually, legitimately, truly be in love with Simon.*

I could not figure out if this was a great thing or a really terrible thing. Because Oregon Rule aside, I still didn't know how serious Simon was about me. Yes, we were "into each other," but that could mean anything from "I enjoy having a friends with benefits situation with you" to "I have a huge crush on you." I really didn't know if it included "I might actually be in love with you."

Simon's eyes moved over the crowd until he found mine. He held my gaze as he sang.

Fucking hell.

I had to get out of here. I knew I was supposed to be flirting with a stranger, but I just didn't have it in me. Not with the weight of my current realization. I made my way to the greenroom. I could tune my guitar for the next twenty minutes. Review lyrics. Put on more makeup.

Contemplate being in love with Simon.

I pushed open the door of the greenroom to find Brooklyn and Evan from Voluntary Commitment speaking in raised voices, practically nose to nose. Colton stood up from the couch and approached both of them, saying something about now not being the time to do this. Tate was nowhere to be seen.

I froze. No one even looked up at me—they were too involved in whatever was going on. I watched as Brooklyn spun on her heel and stomped into the attached bathroom, slamming the door behind her. I slowly backed out of the room and closed the door behind me.

Apparently the tension Voluntary Commitment had onstage was real. I didn't know what they were fighting about, but I definitely didn't think it was a good idea for me to hang out in the greenroom while they did it. I made my way to the back door of the venue and stepped into the night. I could hear Simon still singing about the siren pulling him down. I stared up at the sky.

Fuck.

CHAPTER 24

Waffle Magic and Sound Check

JULY 31: REDDING, CALIFORNIA

SIMON

When we got home last night, I found a private moment and confessed to Marlowe that I had completely failed at flirting with someone else. She gave an exaggerated sigh of relief and told me she had also failed.

Thank god. I knew it was my idea for us to "see other people," so to speak, but it turns out that I did not want to. There was also a small part of me that was terrified that Marlowe actually would meet someone she liked better than me. Which I knew was dumb and insecure, but there was a part of me that couldn't quite believe someone as cool and talented and funny and beautiful as Marlowe would be into *me*.

Everyone from Voluntary Commitment was quiet when we got back to the Airbnb, but the rest of us were wired. Ducky smiled at the other band members as they were putting down their gear.

"Hey, do you guys want to play Smash Bros?"

Brooklyn shook her head and went straight to her room. Evan frowned after her, then turned around and walked out the door, his phone in hand. Tate and Colton both rolled their eyes.

"No thanks," Tate said.

The next half hour was spent listening to the other band members slam doors and occasionally snip at each other, and when Evan got back, we could hear a heated conversation happening.

The rest of us had a whispered conversation about how strained things felt with the other band, but there wasn't really anything we could do about it, so we let it go. Then we had an insane Smash Bros tournament where Aaron smoked all of us.

In the morning, Felix had found a waffle maker, and in an uncharacteristic show of affection, he was making waffles for everyone. Rose was mixing more batter, and I had just sat down at the table when Marlowe came in the front door with two grocery bags.

"Toppings, bitches!" she said. She was wearing a shorts and combat boots combo that I loved, and a loose tank top over a sports bra, her hair in two space buns. She smiled at me, and my heart felt like it was going to explode.

She might be the love of my life, I thought.

And then I immediately panicked and shoved that thought as far away as possible because we still had a week left of the tour and now was not the time for life-changing revelations.

"What did you get?" I asked.

Marlowe lifted the bags onto the counter. "Basically anything you would put on toast and anything you would put on ice cream," she said.

I stood and peeked into one of the bags. Whipped

cream, chocolate syrup, two different types of jam, Nutella…

I reached in and pulled a small container out. "Did you get sprinkles?" I asked.

"Fuck yeah I got sprinkles," Marlowe replied. She flashed a smile at me, and my chest tightened again.

Love of my life.

Ducky walked in and peeked into the bags. "You're so good at buying waffle toppings," she said. She turned to Felix and added, "And you're so good at making waffles."

"You're so good at giving compliments about waffles," Marlowe said to Ducky. Then she turned to me. "And you're probably good at eating waffles."

"Who's good at eating waffles?" Jem asked, walking into the room.

"All of us, probably," Ducky replied. "Are the others awake?"

"Voluntary Commitment all left somewhere earlier," Felix said. "And Aaron is on a run, and I don't know where Wendy is."

"Wendy is right here," came a voice from the stairs.

The next few minutes was a chaotic shuffling around the kitchen, grabbing plates, washing silverware, setting out all of the things Marlowe had bought. Aaron came in and shouted with glee at the breakfast feast being laid out, then ran off to shower.

And suddenly, watching my band mates and my tour mates bantering and passing things around and sitting down to eat, I saw how lucky I was to have it all.

I had a lot of little moments of gratitude any time we went on tour. Small glimmers of joy when the audience was jumping around in the pit, or when me and the guys were locked in to the music, when playing the guitar made me feel immortal. Loud moments of magic.

This was different. Sure, the room was technically loud right now. But the magic was a quieter, surer kind. The kind that anchors you in place. That lets you know that you're right where you belong.

How the hell did I get so fucking lucky?

"Simon, sit down!" Wendy called out, and I lowered myself into the chair beside him.

"Okay, here's the rule!" Ducky shouted. "Everyone has to have a traditional waffle and an insane, sugar-loaded, cardiac arrest, diabetes waffle."

"Can we start with the second one?" Aaron said, walking into the room, his hair still wet from his shower.

"Absolutely," Ducky replied.

"I even got maraschino cherries!" Marlowe said. She was lifting one out of the jar to lower into her mouth, and you'd think I'd be used to how hot she was by now, but I was not.

Wendy grabbed the jar. "Wait, hang on, I have a party trick for this! Give me a stem!"

"Ooohh, Marlowe is good at this," I said.

Wendy turned and stared at me. "How do you know that?"

Uh.

"Because she did it once, at one of our first shows," I said.

I avoided Marlowe's eyes, but joined in the applause when she pulled the cherry stem out of her mouth, a perfect knot in its center.

ALL OF US felt vaguely sick after stuffing ourselves with waffles all morning, but I'd do it again in a heartbeat. We hadn't heard from Voluntary Commitment all day, but when we got to sound check at the venue, they were already there, and *noticeably* not talking to each other. You could cut the tension with a knife.

The rest of us quietly brought our gear inside and tried to like, be invisible? It wasn't just that they needed complete quiet for sound check—I think all of us just felt like a bomb was about to go off, and we were trying to avoid the trigger. Colton seemed particularly aggressive on the drums as the sound guy checked his levels.

"Do you guys wanna play through something for a minute?" the sound guy asked.

Voluntary Commitment launched into one of their songs, but it was messy, chaotic. After a moment, Brooklyn paused.

"Could I get more bass in my wedge?" Brooklyn called out.

"We all know you like bass in your wedge," Colton said from behind his drum set. It sounded like a joke, but there wasn't any humor in his voice when he said it.

"Whoa!" Tate exclaimed.

Brooklyn whirled around and glared at Colton. "Fuck you, Colton!"

Colton stood up, but Tate was there in a second, steadying him with a hand on his shoulder.

"Why don't you mind your business?!" Evan said, whipping his bass off.

Brooklyn turned to glare at him, too. "Oh, now you speak up! Fuck you, too, actually!"

Evan lifted his hands in surrender. "Babe, calm down—"

"Do *not* call me babe! And I won't calm down!"

I watched Tate look from band member to band member. "Hey, everyone just chill…"

Colton threw Tate's hand off his shoulder. "You can't

just tell people to chill, Tate! That's not going to solve shit! Fuck this." He threw his drum sticks onto the ground and stormed off.

Evan watched him go, then followed after him, calling his name.

Tate and Brooklyn stood in silence for a moment. Then Tate took a tentative step forward.

Brooklyn stared at the ground, then whipped her guitar off. She made her way over to its case.

"I'm going home," she said. "You guys can figure your own shit out." I saw her angrily swipe a tear away as she stood up. She made her way to the back door and slammed it behind her. Tate sank down into a crouch, his head in his hands.

Queen Anne and the Boy Scouts stood frozen in place. A few of us exchanged worried glances. Finally, Aaron stepped forward.

"Hey, is…is everything all right, man?"

Tate looked up at him. "No," he replied. Then he stood up and walked out of the door.

No one knew what to say. Finally, the sound guy broke the silence. "So I'm Van," he said. "Do you guys wanna set up?"

"Sure," Jem said. "Ducky, will you help me take apart these drums?"

We all stepped into action, putting Voluntary Commitment's gear to the side of the stage and setting up our own. Aaron looked toward the back door with a worried expression. "Do you think they're coming back?"

Van shrugged. "Apparently the guitarist and the bassist were hooking up and everyone just found out about it yesterday. I don't know if anyone is coming back. Can y'all play long enough to cover for them?"

"We've got it," Jem said.

"Good," Van nodded. "I guess we can be ready for them to come back, but…" he glanced at the back door. "I don't think that's happening."

CHAPTER 25

Until We Get Home
AUGUST 1: SACRAMENTO, CALIFORNIA

MARLOWE

"Okay, tour meeting!" Jem called. Last night's show was a little rough around the edges, but we made it work. Tonight we were playing Sacramento, and we'd just finished sound check. It felt easy after the drama of yesterday's.

The rest of us gathered around Jem on stage. Her lips were pressed in a stern line. "All right," she said. "I know we've only got two stops left on this tour. Only one more after this one. But after witnessing Voluntary Commitment's…disintegration yesterday, I feel the need to reiterate The Oregon Rule."

Ducky rolled her eyes. "We knowwww," she said. "None of us are fucking. Calm down."

Jem turned to her. "I'm being serious, Ducky."

"Jem is right," Felix said. He stood with his hands in his pockets, worrying his lip ring with his tongue. He looked up at all of us. "Dating between band mates and tour mates fucks everything up. But more importantly, it fucks everyone over. Don't do that."

My stomach sank. I couldn't look bring myself to look at Simon. I felt like my whole body was filled with lead. I kept thinking about this wonderful little group we had—all the fun we've had on tour. Not just on stage, but at the beach and in the Redwoods, and in Airbnb's and on ropes courses.

I didn't want to lose that.

But I didn't want to lose Simon either.

THE SHOW WAS FINE, and everyone was exhausted when we got back. We were staying at another Airbnb with a backyard, and I watched Simon step out of the back door. I waited a few minutes before following him, feeling grateful we had someplace it was easy to slip away to. He was sitting in a chair out on the tiny patch of lawn, gazing up at the night sky. I took the chair next to him.

"Hi," I said.

He turned to me, and even in the dim light, I could see his eyes were troubled. My stomach sank.

"I've been thinking," he said, turning his attention back to the sky.

"Same," I replied.

I waited for Simon to continue, but he didn't say anything for a long time. "Yesterday morning," he said. "When Felix made waffles. I had this moment…" I watched his Adam's apple bob as he swallowed. He turned to me. "I really really like you, Marlowe."

I wanted so badly for him to say more about how much he liked me. I wanted him to say he didn't care what anyone thought or what rules we were breaking, that he wanted to be with me. But I could tell from his tone of voice that this conversation was probably going in another direction.

And if it was, I knew that was the right choice. I knew we should stop, and I didn't think I could resist Simon if he said we shouldn't. But I didn't want to let the moment pass by without saying something about how I felt.

"I like you, too, Simon," I whispered. "A lot. Like, a lot a lot."

Simon looked pained. "Yesterday morning…" he continued. "I was looking around at all of us, and it was such a simple thing, just eating breakfast together, but I just…I really love this little tour family we've created. I love that we all get along and have fun together. I…I don't want to ruin that."

Part of me knew this was coming, but tears stung my eyes anyway. "Are you breaking up with me?" I asked. When I looked up at Simon's face, he looked miserable.

"Just…for now," he said. "Just until we get home."

"When you go to Colorado for two weeks," I mumbled.

"As long as you're not coming with us on tour, I can ask you out again in six days."

I knew it wasn't a "real" break up. We were just… taking a break. But it still hurt, and a tear fell down my cheek anyway.

"Oh, sweetheart," Simon exclaimed. "Come here."

I sniffled and got out of my chair. I threw a leg over Simon's so that I could straddle him, and let him wrap his arms around me. I buried my face in his shoulder. I let his spicy, citrus-y scent enfold me, his body warm beneath me.

"Am I allowed to hate breaking up?" I asked, my voice muffled. "Even if it's temporary?"

Simon let out a gentle laugh. "I hope so, because I also hate it," he said.

I sat up and looked at him. "Okay," I said. "We are temporarily breaking up. Emphasis on the *temporary*."

"And when we get back to Alameda, I will ask you out so hard," Simon replied.

"You're pretty good at doing things 'so hard,'" I replied, smirking despite my sadness.

Simon laughed out loud. "One last kiss?" he asked.

"One last kiss until six days from now," I replied, and leaned my head down.

Simon's lips were soft and warm, moving tenderly against mine. Within seconds, I felt my breath quicken. My hips rolled, seeking connection, and Simon's grip grew tighter. He let out a tiny moan, and I chased after it, kissing him harder.

Slam!

I lifted my head in time to see Ducky standing by the back door. I scrambled off Simon's lap, but it was too late. She had definitely seen us.

"Ducky…" I said.

She was frozen on the spot, her mouth hanging open. But in the next moment, she folded her arms and glared at us.

Simon looked at me, then back at Ducky. "Should I… should I go inside?"

"Yeah, why don't you do that," Ducky said, her voice furious.

Simon cast one apologetic look at me, then made his way to the back door. Ducky didn't even glance at him. As soon as he was gone, she marched over to me.

"I am not a violent person," she said. "But I want to punch both of you in the face right now."

"I'm sorry," I said, my voice sounding small.

"I literally asked you," Ducky said. "I literally asked

you what was going on between the two of you, *weeks* ago, in Coos Bay, and you said you weren't interested in him."

"I know."

"Was that a lie?"

"No!" I exclaimed, some part of me still trying to save this. But Ducky raised her eyebrows at me, so I swallowed and said, "Yes."

She glared. "How long has this been going on?"

I swallowed, looking at the ground. "Since Portland," I whispered. But then I thought of our kiss in the greenroom days before Portland. "Or maybe...Salem."

"So the two of you were just going to, what? Lie to everyone for the rest of the tour?"

I shook my head, desperate to defend myself. "We were literally breaking up when you came out here," I said. "We felt really awful about it."

"Sure didn't look like breaking up," Ducky said.

"I promise. Please. It wasn't..." I struggled to put my thoughts into words. "We were talking about how much the tour means to both of us. How much the bands mean to us. And we decided we needed to stop...whatever it is we were doing. At least until we get back to Alameda. We were trying to do the right thing. Please, Ducky."

Ducky glared at me. "So now what am I supposed to do?! Go back inside and act like I didn't just find you two dry humping in a chair?"

My voice was tiny when I replied. "Yes?"

Ducky shook her head and started pacing. "This is so shitty," she said. "Do you understand how shitty this is?"

"Please, Ducky," I said. "We just have two more stops on the tour. Just six more days. And Simon and I are stopping. We broke up. What you saw was a goodbye kiss. I don't...I don't want to ruin the last week of the tour with something that won't be a thing anymore. Will you please, please not tell anyone?"

Ducky stopped and glared at me again, then looked up at the sky. I watched as she thought through the options— be honest with the rest of our tour mates and risk blowing everything up, or keep the secret, which was shitty, but would preserve the tour. She literally growled in frustration. Finally, she looked at me.

"You're stopping?" she asked. "You promise you broke up?"

I nodded, hope swelling in my chest. "I promise."

Ducky studied my face, then finally she nodded. "Fine," she said. "But this is the shittiest thing you have ever done."

I was still aching with shame, but relief flooded me. "Thank you, Ducky," I said.

"I'm not over this," Ducky said. "You and I aren't okay. I'll keep your secret, but this is gonna take a while to come back from." She turned and walked back to the house.

I collapsed into the chair and stayed there until I was sure my tears had stopped.

CHAPTER 26

There's Something About a Greenroom

AUGUST 4: SANTA CRUZ, CALIFORNIA

SIMON

It had been three miserable days since Marlowe and I "broke up" and I hated every single one of them. Even though it was temporary, it was still miserable.

Marlowe had texted me that Ducky was willing to not tell anyone, which was a relief, even though it also made me feel incredibly guilty. It wasn't fair to Ducky to have to carry our secret, especially since she wasn't involved in it at all. She didn't break the Oregon Rule. She shouldn't have to be an accessory to our crime.

But I also knew how awful everything would be if she *did* tell. We were so close to being done with the tour…we just had to make it a few more days.

I wish to god she hadn't walked in on me and Marlowe in the backyard. (Walked "out" on us?)

To add to my anxiety, tonight was the night that the Bumbershoot rep was coming to the show. Getting to play a festival like Bumbershoot could be a huge deal for both the Boy Scouts of Atlantis and Queen Anne. The stakes felt high. During sound check, there was a nervous buzzing energy filling the room, and Jem and Felix were both more intense than usual, making sure we sounded as tight as possible.

The Boy Scouts were on in about twenty minutes, so I made my way to the greenroom to replace one of my guitar strings. The room was like so many greenrooms in so many venues—dim lighting, shitty thrift store couches, stickers from previous bands on the walls and tables. I remembered Ducky's suggestion that someone start another Instagram. It could be called "Meet me in the Greenroom." There was just something kind of magical about venue greenrooms, even the shitty ones. Like venue bathrooms, only weirdly exclusive. A VIP look behind the curtain. This greenroom had brocade velvet curtains on the walls, tied back with thick gold rope. Probably left over from when the space was a theatre.

I was just tightening the tuning peg for my new string when I heard Marlowe's voice.

"Ducky was right, someone should start an Instagram of venue greenrooms," she said, looking around.

I smiled at her from my spot on the couch. "I was literally just thinking the same thing."

We stayed like that for a moment, her standing in the doorway, me sitting on the couch, just smiling at each other. She was wearing her tutu/fishnets/combat boots combo again, her hair in a braided crown.

God, I loved her.

I shifted my attention back to my guitar, because now was not the time. Marlowe came and sat on the couch next to me. She glanced at the door, then back at me.

"Did you…did you need something?" I asked.

"Just saying hi," Marlowe replied. "Why, do you think we shouldn't be alone together?"

I swallowed. "It's probably fine."

I lifted my guitar and played the first few notes of "Siren," pausing to tune the new string. In the back of my mind, I wondered what the hell I was doing. But I continued playing softly, quietly, focusing on the guitar in my lap.

"Her siren song…I'm all at sea, she's calling me. I know it's wrong. My sailor's thoughts, all tied in—"

But then, despite everything, Marlowe leaned in to kiss me and I stopped being able to make rational decisions. I tossed my guitar onto the couch next to me, then pulled Marlowe into my arms. She practically crawled into my lap, her tongue licking into my mouth, her hands in my hair. How had I lived without this for even one *day*?

One of my hands reached up to clutch at her breast, and she let out a hungry sound in the back of her throat.

"What the fuck?!"

Marlowe and I flew apart. I looked up to see Jem standing in the doorway, looking shocked. I was frozen in place on the couch, and Marlowe jumped to her feet.

"What's going on?" another voice said, and Wendy peeked around behind her.

"They were fucking making out is what's going on," Jem replied.

Felix walked in beside Jem. "They were what?!"

And then suddenly everyone was in the greenroom, staring at us. There was no way we could have denied it. Marlowe's red lipstick was smeared and I'm sure some of it was on my face. And Jem had literally seen us—she had seen with her own eyes what we were doing.

Jem folded her arms and glared at us. "Marlowe and Simon were in this greenroom, *kissing. Intensely.*"

"What the goddamn fuck?!" Felix demanded. He looked more furious than I'd ever seen him. "Bumbershoot is out there right now. *Right now.*"

"You couldn't have followed the rules for once in your life, Marlowe?" Jem demanded.

"I…I know," Marlowe faltered.

Ducky stepped forward. "You said you stopped!" she hissed.

Jem turned to her. "You knew about this?!"

"We broke up!" Marlowe explained.

"Then what the hell were you making out for?!" Ducky yelled.

But Jem shook her head at Ducky. "Sorry, can we go back to the part where you knew about this?"

Ducky took a breath. After one quick glance at Marlowe, she turned to Jem and said, "I caught them kissing in the backyard in Sacramento. They made me promise to keep it a secret because—" She turned to Marlowe and me and emphasized the last part of her sentence. "*Because they said they were stopping.*"

"We were!" I say. "This was just…I don't know…something happened and—"

Felix cut me off. "We had one day left of this tour. You couldn't have waited one more day?!"

"Oh, it's been going on since Salem," Ducky said. Her voice was filled with venom, and when I glanced at Marlowe, she looked crushed.

"Felix…" I started.

But Felix just glared. I'd never seen him look so upset. "No," he said, then turned and walked out of the room. Wendy gave me a troubled look, then followed after him. My gaze moved to Aaron, and the expression on his face devastated me. He looked so hurt, so betrayed. Aaron was one of the purest souls I knew, and I felt like I had stomped all over his friendship. He took a deep breath, then turned and followed Felix and Wendy.

"Why did you do this?" Rose asked quietly. She had her arms wrapped around herself, which made her seem even smaller than usual. She looked up at Marlowe.

"Rose…"

But Rose shook her head. "The Oregon Rule is important to Felix. But it's there for all of us. Even if it's difficult or painful or…" Rose's eyes filled with tears, and she covered her mouth with her hand before running out of the room.

Jem glared at me and Marlowe. "I'm going to go make sure Rose is okay," she said. "And also, I can't even explain to you how much this sucks. Fuck you both. Fuck you for disregarding everyone else's feelings, for betraying everyone's friendship, and for shitting all over this tour." She stared at the floor. "Of all the goddamn nights for you to shit all over the tour. Bumbershoot." She lifted her eyes and spun on Ducky. "And fuck *you* for keeping this a secret."

Her words knocked the wind out of me. Not just because they were so intense, but because I knew they were true. Jem spun on her heel and walked out of the room, and Ducky stared at the ground, looking angry and wounded, before leaving as well.

I turned to Marlowe, but she just stood there. Then she covered her face with her hands and burst into tears.

I stood. "Marlowe, sweetheart."

But when I touched her arm, she shrugged me off. She ran out of the room, leaving me to collapse onto the couch and hang my head in my hands.

∾

THAT NIGHT'S SHOW WAS, without a doubt, the worst show I had ever played in my life. I didn't know if the audience could sense how much tension there was between all of us onstage, but I would have been shocked if they didn't notice. Wendy drummed harder than usual, which also meant faster than usual in some places, so our rhythms were all off. Felix and Aaron and I often played off of each other during shows, both musically and with banter, but neither of them would even meet my eye. I sang most of our set with my eyes closed—I wasn't getting anything from my bandmates, and I couldn't stand the idea of seeing Marlowe or anyone else from Queen Anne in the crowd. I needed to just disappear into the music. It was the only place I could think of to go, but for once, it didn't make me feel better.

Queen Anne's set wasn't much better. Jem chose all of their angriest songs and practically shouted through all of them. Rose seemed near tears the whole time, and Ducky looked ready to punch through her drums. Marlowe didn't look at me at all the whole time she was onstage, and her solos were intense and chaotic.

Thank god we were staying at a motel tonight. It was already going to be hard enough dealing with my three bandmates—I couldn't imagine trying to navigate Queen Anne's feelings if we were all sharing an Airbnb. And the thought of spending a night in the same place as Marlowe again was torture. I wanted so desperately to go find her, to pull her into my arms, to assure her that we could figure all of this out together.

But I couldn't think of anything that would upset everyone more.

None of us talked about the show as we packed up our gear. No discussion of Bumbershoot or Marlowe and me or how we'd played. Guilt burned through me.

Marlowe didn't look at me in the motel parking lot as we each went to our rooms. I wordlessly took a shower, brushed my teeth, and went to bed. Right before I closed my eyes, my phone lit up with a text from Marlowe.

MARLOWE: I'm sorry.

CHAPTER 27
The Drive

AUGUST 5: SANTA CRUZ, CALIFORNIA TO
OAKLAND, CALIFORNIA

MARLOWE

Packing up this morning was a tense affair. We probably could have just all gone home last night—it was only about an hour and a half from Santa Cruz to Alameda. But we wouldn't have gotten home until three or four in the morning.

In the parking lot, everyone quietly lifted their gear into each car. I couldn't bring myself to look at Simon. I think we all would have been kind of sad anyway, since it was the end of the tour. But the weight of the broken Oregon Rule hung over all of us like a storm cloud.

Correction: the weight of Simon and I breaking the Oregon Rule hung over all of us. It wasn't just broken. *We* broke it.

Finally, all of us stood on the asphalt, instruments and gear and luggage all loaded up. Jem looked at all of us.

"It's been a pleasure to play this tour with you, Boy Scouts," she said. I hid a smile despite the atmosphere.

Only Jem could make a compliment sound so militaristic. But then she turned to me.

"Marlowe, you're riding with me. Ducky, take Rose in Marlowe's car." She addressed the rest of the group. "I'd like to propose a end-of-tour celebration when the Boy Scouts of Atlantis return from Colorado. We'll be in touch. Drive safe."

And with that, Jem made her way to her Subaru. I stole a glance at Simon, but he was staring at the ground as he walked toward the van. Everyone exchanged goodbyes, and I tossed my keys to Ducky before sliding into the passenger's seat next to Jem.

I had a feeling I was about to be thoroughly scolded. I wished I could tell Jem that I didn't need it—I already felt bad enough. But I didn't think it would make any difference.

As soon as we were on the highway, Jem turned to me.

"I want to understand," she said. "What you were thinking."

I swallowed. "I don't know if I can," I replied. "I don't know if I *was* thinking."

Jem was quiet for a long time. "Who started it?"

I tried to think back throughout the tour, all the little moments that led to Simon and I falling into each other. But I couldn't even say who started our first kiss. "It was pretty mutual," I replied.

"I guess that makes sense," Jem nodded, sounding resigned. "You're well suited."

I turned to her, suddenly filled with anger. "We're 'well-suited'?! Then why the hell are you mad about us getting together?"

Jem's fingers tightened on the steering wheel. "Marlowe, no one is mad about you getting together."

I threw my hands into the air. "Then what the hell is the problem?!"

"The problem is that you lied, Marlowe!" Jem retorted. I didn't think I'd ever heard her yell like this before, and it made me sink into my seat. "Both you and Simon!" she continued. "And don't you dare give me any bullshit about 'not lying' just because you didn't outright say 'we're not together.' You lied by omission, and you probably straight up lied, too."

I couldn't think of anything to say to that.

"So why did you do it?" Jem repeated.

And I couldn't help it, tears stung my eyes. I shook my head. "I didn't mean to hurt anyone," I said. "Truly."

Jem sighed. "I know, Marlowe. But I asked you why you did it."

I stared out of the window. A hundred images moved through my mind. Simon looking up at me from behind his guitar in the Redwoods, when all of us were complimenting him. His eyes as he sang "Sirens" directly to me. The way the music took over him when he was onstage, no matter what he was playing or singing. Simon holding me on the ropes course, assuring me that he would keep me safe. I thought of his lips and hands and body moving against me, the noises he made, the way he looked at me. Even when we were "breaking up," he spoke about his band mates with so much love—it was so clear that he treated his friendships as sacred. We made each other laugh, and flirting with him was more fun than I'd ever had in my life. And there was his absurd desire to follow the rules—even when breaking the Oregon Rule made us both so happy, he still wanted to do the right thing. It guided so much of who he was, and even though I was a rebel at heart, something about that quality in him spoke to my soul.

I struggled to put all of that into words. "Because… because Simon is a great songwriter and performer. Because he has an Instagram of venue bathrooms. Because he's funny and brave and caring and creative and passionate. Because he smelled so fucking good all the time that I could hardly stand it. Because he knows who he is and he lives by his values."

I am in love with Simon, I thought. Again. I already knew it…I'd known it for at least a week. But listing out all those reasons just made it all the more clear in my mind. I leaned forward and put my head in my hands.

When Jem replied, her voice was quiet. "Why didn't you just tell someone? Any of us?"

"Because I was scared out of my mind, Jem!" I replied, lifting my head. "Because we had such a great thing going on tour and I was afraid that telling people about us would ruin it."

"Marlowe, you know I love you, but you can't live your life in fear."

For some reason, that made me furious (again). "That's not fair," I said. "How do you know I was 'living my life in fear'?" I put air quotes around the phrase.

"Because you literally just said you were scared out of your mind, Marlowe."

Okay, she had a point. But I still wasn't done. "Well, the Oregon Rule itself is made out of fear!" I exclaimed. Which I originally said out of anger, but…I actually had a good point. "Why can't we just trust each other to handle whatever goes wrong? Why don't any of us believe we're mature enough to deal with breakups or hookups or whatever? Fights happen even when people *aren't* dating!"

"The stakes are higher when romance and sex are part of—"

"You know I'm right, Jem."

Jem kept her eyes on the road, not replying. I was suddenly exhausted. I was carrying so much anger and so much heartbreak and so much guilt. The last 24 hours had been the longest of my life. I leaned my head against the window and let my tears fall.

A full fifteen minutes later, I looked up at Jem. To my shock, I saw her swipe away a tear, and my chest squeezed painfully. Jem was so guarded most of the time, I almost didn't know what to do with this display of vulnerability. But I was flooded with love for this friend I'd known for so long. "No, Jem! Why are *you* crying?" I exclaimed.

Jem didn't look at me when she replied. "Because the whole thing is shitty. Because you're right, the Oregon Rule was probably made out of fear and we all probably could have figured out how to handle you and Simon getting together on the tour. But the whole situation was just…it set everyone up to fail, and all of us *did* fail. You and Simon missed out on being together in front of all of us, and then you kept a secret, and you made Ducky keep that secret, too. And that was another betrayal. This whole thing could have all been friendship and romance, and instead it was lies and secrecy."

"I'm so sorry, Jem," I said, my voice watery.

"Thank you," she said.

"I…I don't say it a lot to you," I continued. "But I love the fuck out of you. You mean so much to me. Queen Anne means so much to me. Not just because of the music, but the friendship too. I'm so sorry I risked that."

"I love you, too, Marlowe," Jem replied. The sincerity in her voice moved me to tears *again*. How could I have any more crying left in me?

"We'll figure it out," Jem added. "I'm still mad, and I think the others are too, but I want to figure it out."

"Me, too," I said.

We drove the rest of the way home in silence.

CHAPTER 28
The Walk

AUGUST 5: SANTA CRUZ, CALIFORNIA TO OAKLAND, CALIFORNIA

SIMON

The drive home with the guys was one of the quietest of my life. It wasn't a long drive, but I was acutely aware of the silence. The whole time I kept thinking about how we all lived together, so counting down the minutes until we got home wasn't even going to be helpful. I imagined the tension would just continue. As soon as we got to our duplex, everyone brought their gear and luggage inside, and then Felix and Wendy disappeared into their rooms.

So I was right.

Aaron stood awkwardly in the living room for a moment. Then he looked at me. "Hey, do you want to go on a walk or something?"

I blinked at him. That wasn't at all what I was expecting. "Sure," I said.

We walked a few blocks without talking. Without thinking about it, we were walking toward our old elementary school. One of the reasons I liked going on tour was because at home, the sights that surrounded me were so deeply familiar that I got tired of them sometimes. I'd spent my entire life in the Bay Area. The trees and cracks in the sidewalk and BART schedules were all familiar to me.

"Hey do you remember third grade?" Aaron asked.

I gave him a quizzical look. "Not…all of it," I replied. "But I remember third grade."

"There was a day," Aaron continued. "When Xander Thompson got basically beat up by a bunch of fourth graders. At recess. It was raining like crazy."

I knew the day Aaron was talking about. It had loomed large in my memory for a lot of my childhood, but I hadn't thought about it in years.

"I remember," I said.

Aaron nodded. "Xander was out in the field, crying, just laying there when the bell rang. I remember his nose was bleeding. And you and me stayed out there with him for a long time. Until he felt okay enough to go back inside. We were soaked by the time we brought him in to the office. And we both got detention for staying out after the recess bell."

"Which was totally unfair," I replied. I remembered the deep sense of injustice I had felt as an eight-year-old. When Aaron and I had tried to explain what had happened to Xander, we got reprimanded for "tattling." Xander had been sitting there, bruises already forming on his cheek, his nose bleeding, and the kids who did it didn't even get called in to talk to the principal.

"What made you think of that?" I asked.

"I've been thinking about rules lately," Aaron replied.

Ah.

"Me, too," I replied. Neither of us said anything more for another block. Then Aaron cleared his throat.

"I understand why you broke the rule about staying out past the recess bell in third grade. You did it for the same reason I did. Because Xander was hurt and you cared about him."

I nodded. I couldn't quite remember if I'd been the same rule-follower then that I was now. I'm pretty sure I didn't think at all about the bell ringing on that day with Xander, or being late to class. It didn't even occur to me that we would get in trouble.

"I like to think that's true," I replied.

Aaron's voice wavered a little bit when he spoke next. "Did you break the Oregon Rule because you cared about Marlowe or because you didn't care about us?"

I stopped in my tracks, and Aaron stopped next to me. "Aaron," I said. "I care so much about you, and Felix, and Wendy. Like, so much."

"And Marlowe?"

My heart thudded in my chest. I stared at the sidewalk. "I care about Marlowe a lot," I replied.

"How?" Aaron asked.

"Huh?"

"How do you care about her? Like, is it lust or like or love?"

I blew my breath out slowly, trying not to panic. "It might be…it's at least like. It could be love. If it's not already, it's on its way."

Aaron nodded and resumed walking. We fell into step next to each other. "Thanks for answering my questions," he said. "I think I needed to like, understand. All of it was so surprising that I didn't know what to think. I didn't know if you really had feelings for Marlowe, or if you just…completely screwed the tour and the band over because you thought someone was hot."

I hated that Aaron thought I was even capable of treating our band mates so callously. "Definitely not the second one," I said. "Not ever the second one. I fucking love you, man. And Felix and Wendy. The Boy Scouts of Atlantis…this band is hella important to me. I hate that you guys were collateral damage to my feelings for Marlowe."

"I'm gonna be more real with you than I've ever been," Aaron said. His tone was deadly serious, filling my stomach with dread.

"Okay," I said.

"I think you and Marlowe are really great together," he said.

Relief ballooned inside of me. "Thanks," I breathed.

"I have more things to say."

I nodded.

"I know you say you care about the band," Aaron continued. "And I believe you. But you didn't act like it on this tour. Feelings don't mean as much as actions, Simon. If you say you love us, but then go behind our backs and keep something like this a secret, completely breaking a rule we made to keep us together, that doesn't…it makes it hard to believe you."

This was the most serious I'd ever seen Aaron. I'd known him almost my entire life—I didn't have many memories from before Aaron and I were friends. He and I had had some deep conversations over the years, but I'd never heard him drop so much truth so eloquently.

I knew he was right. Secretly breaking the Oregon Rule with Marlowe was shitty because it was a big middle finger to these other people that I cared about.

"When did you get so wise?" I asked.

Aaron chuckled. "It's because I'm dumb as shit about a lot of other things," he replied.

I sighed. "How bad did I fuck up?" I asked. I knew Aaron would be honest.

"Pretty bad," he replied.

"Is Colorado gonna suck?"

Aaron thought for a moment. "I don't think I can hold a grudge. I don't know if I even want to. Now that I know why you did it—now that I know you don't hate us or whatever—I feel a little better. I don't know about Wendy and Felix, though."

I nodded. "Thank you, Aaron."

He nodded, then stopped and pulled me into a hug. I was crushed against his chest, but I didn't give a damn. We stood like that for a moment, and I was flooded with gratitude. "Dudes should hug like this way more often," I said, my voice muffled.

Aaron laughed as we pulled apart. "Let's go home," he said. "Even if it sucks."

I nodded. I didn't know what was going to happen between me and Marlowe when the Boy Scouts got back from Colorado. I had no idea what was going to happen between me and Marlowe *today*. We hadn't talked since her text last night. I knew she and the rest of Queen Anne must have been getting to their Victorian-home-turned-apartment any second now, if they hadn't already arrived. She was only a ten-minute drive away. I could even walk it if I was desperate.

But I didn't want to talk to her until I had figured my shit out.

CHAPTER 29

The Seaside Cure

AUGUST 12-13: MARINA, CALIFORNIA

MARLOWE

The day after we got back to Alameda, after Jem and Rose and Ducky all disappeared into their rooms, I texted a friend who works at an RV park in Marina, near Santa Cruz. She got me a deal on a week-long stay at one of the mini "cottages" they have, so I packed my guitar and my suitcase and drove out there to clear my head.

And to give my roommates/bandmates some space. I thought we all needed it. I'd spent the last week going on long walks on the beach, playing my guitar, and binge-watching a handful of shows when I couldn't stand another second of self-reflection.

Now I was standing on the cottage porch, my cell phone in my hand, trying to figure out what to say to Simon Burroughs when I called him in two minutes.

We hadn't spoken since the end of the tour. Part of me felt bad for cutting him off so abruptly, but he hadn't reached out to me either. I had a feeling both of us sensed the need for space. For just a minute. But now

I was ready to say a few things and I wanted to decide a few things with him. I had texted to ask if I could call him and he told me to give him two minutes, which gave me two minutes to feel like I was going to throw up.

Finally, after at least three minutes because I was nervous, I pulled up Simon's name and dialed.

"Hey," he answered.

Warmth flooded my body at the sound of his voice. "Hey," I breathed.

"It's…good to hear from you," Simon said. "Your voice, I mean. I missed the sound of your voice. And your words, too. Like, both the content of what you say is important, and is something I missed, and also the way your voice sounds."

I bit back a smile. "I missed you, too." A pause. "How's Colorado?"

"A little bit…tense, but the shows have been going well. How are things in Alameda?"

"I'm actually in Marina right now," I said. "I needed a minute."

"Taking the seaside cure?" Simon teased. I could hear his smile as he asked.

"Exactly," I laughed.

"And is it working?"

I looked out to where the sun was setting beyond the dunes. Later tonight, I would walk along the shoreline in the moonlight like I had the last five nights, the soft rush of ocean waves echoing in my ears. "I think it is."

We were both silent for a moment.

"So," Simon said. "You wanted to talk?"

I swallowed. "Yes," I said. "I think…Simon, I really like you."

"But…?"

"Not a 'but,'" I rushed to say. "Unless you have a 'but,' which means this whole convo is gonna go differently."

"I don't have a 'but,'" Simon said. "Well, I mean, I *do*, but not a…grammatical one."

My heart swelled. "I like you, Simon," I said. "*And* my friendships with my bandmates are really important to me. I need to repair those relationships before anything can happen between you and me. Or, anything else, I mean."

I heard Simon blow out a puff of air before replying. "That is actually incredible news, because I need to do the same thing. I need to get right with Felix and Wendy before I get right with you. We're not going to last otherwise."

I collapsed into one of the chairs on the porch. "Oh thank god," I said.

Simon laughed gently. "Have you been torturing yourself with this? Because I have been."

"Yes," I said emphatically.

"So what now?" Simon asked.

"When do you get back from Colorado?"

"August 20th."

I thought for a moment. "What if we don't talk again until you get back?" I asked. "Give each other a bit of space for just a little while longer, to sort everything out with the other people we love?"

I suddenly realized that I'd just said "other people we love," implying that I also loved *him*, which was true, but also this was not the time. I held my breath.

"That sounds like a great plan," Simon replied. He paused, then added, "I miss you."

My whole body lit up. "I miss you, too," I said. And then I had to end this phone call or I was going to make bigger confessions about just how *much* I missed him. "Talk to you in a week?"

"In a week and a day."

"Bye, Simon."
"Bye, Marlowe."

~

THE NEXT MORNING, I packed up and headed home. I had called a house/band meeting for that night, and wanted to make sure everything was ready. I made sure the living room was tidy and I ordered us pizza. The meal was a little strained, but that was to be expected. When everyone had finished eating, I grabbed my acoustic guitar from my room and came back out.

"So, I've been doing a lot of thinking," I said. Jem, Ducky, and Rose all looked at me expectantly. If I looked too close, I'd be able to see the various levels of hurt and anger in their faces, and I wouldn't be able to finish this thing, so I looked down at the ground.

"I spent all week trying to write a song for you guys," I said. "Something to tell you how much I care about you. But every song I tried to write just turned into some version of this one, so this is…this is me saying how sorry I am."

I plucked the opening notes of John Denver's "My Sweet Lady." I knew it was a love song, but I couldn't create anything as tender, as heartfelt, as honest as this one. By the time I got to the lyrics "close your eyes," I couldn't hold back my tears anymore. But then I heard Rose's clear soft voice start singing, and then Jem's. Then Ducky walked to her drum set and started moving the brushes over the snare in a gentle rhythm. And then *all* of us were crying, and we barely made it to the end of the song. When we did, the room was quiet for a moment, and then Ducky walked out from behind her drum set and said, "Fuck all of you, come *here!*"

I set down my guitar and then collapsed into her arms, and then Rose and Jem joined in, and the four of us stood in our living room, hugging and crying.

Jem finally broke out of our group embrace. "Uggghhh, too many feelings," she said.

"I am so so so sorry," I said. "Everyone. I never meant to hurt any of you, and I'm so sorry I lied. I'm so sorry I risked our friendship and this band by breaking the Oregon Rule."

Ducky shrugged. "Honestly, it might be too strict of a rule. But thank you. For saying that. I super hated the last two weeks when we weren't friends."

"Same!" Rose exclaimed.

"Eh, I can take or leave you bitches," Jem said, but her eyes were still shining with tears.

"I love you guys," I said. "So fucking much. I don't want anything, man or job or friendship or anything, to come between us. I promise to think about you all more, and be better."

"Are you going to keep seeing Simon?" Rose asked.

I sighed. "We agreed to take a break—full no contact —until he gets back from Colorado. He said whatever we have between us won't be sustainable unless everyone else is on board."

"I'm on board," Rose replied, smiling.

"Oh thank god," I breathed. "Ducky? Jem?"

"I approve," Ducky said, "Now that you've apologized and as long as you promise to not be a dick about it."

"No dickery, promise," I replied, crossing my heart. "Jem?"

"First of all, you don't need our approval to date someone. You have full autonomy. But also, thanks for asking, and yes I approve but only if you are fully honest from this day on. No more lies, or secrets, or risking everything else valuable in your life for some guy."

"He's not some guy!" Rose protested.

"Fine, some 'great' guy," Jem said.

"Full honesty," I said. I reached out and squeezed Jem's hand. She wasn't generally an affectionate person, so when she squeezed my hand back, I knew it meant something.

CHAPTER 30

A Waffle Olive Branch

AUGUST 13: GRAND JUNCTION, COLORADO

SIMON

Felix had been giving me the silent treatment for the last week. Or the "I'll only talk to you if necessary and I won't be outright aggressive but our interactions will be minimal" treatment. Aaron and I were back to our old friendship, and Wendy…Wendy seemed to kind of hover uncertainly between the two extremes. He didn't do or say anything particularly mean to me, but he was a little distant.

We had played well at the shows we'd had so far. Felix had vetoed the "Siren" song from our set lists, which was understandable, and actually kind of a relief. I didn't know if I could stand playing it under the current circumstances.

I mostly kept my head down and tried to be the best bandmate possible. I helped everyone with their gear and I was considerate at sound check. I focused on playing and singing well. When we weren't playing shows, I spent a lot of time on walks. Sometimes I'd sit down in a cafe or library or something. But I kind of tried to stay out of my bandmates' way. Give them as much space as I could.

The whole thing had been working so far, even if it sucked. But after my phone call with Marlowe last night, I needed for us all to figure our shit out. Enough time had passed. We needed to talk. Because the polite distance between all of us wasn't sustainable.

So I decided to make us all waffles.

Which was a little insane because we were staying at a motel with no kitchenette or anything, so I had to buy waffle mix and a bowl and measuring cups. And a waffle maker. I figured that would be an investment—we didn't have one at home.

We didn't have a show tonight, so while walking home with all of my purchases, I texted the guys and told them dinner was on me. When I opened the door to our hotel room, Felix frowned at me. Aaron jumped up to help, and Wendy glanced up before returning to his video game.

I realized that I had forgotten plates and utensils, so Aaron ran out to grab some while I was cooking. I'm not much of a cook, but I was able to manage waffles from a box mix. Within twenty minutes, Aaron was back, and I had set up a "waffle bar," complete with toppings, on one of the dressers.

After taking his first bite, Wendy looked up at me. "Thanks for making these," he said.

It wasn't a huge thing to say, but gratitude rushed through me. It was the most genuine connection we'd had in days. "You're welcome," I said. I cleared my throat. "When, um…when you're all done eating, I want to say something. Or talk about something. If we could."

Aaron grinned at me. "I knew you had an ulterior motive for feeding us," he said. I smiled at him. God, I was glad to have him on my side. This would have been even more difficult if I had had to do it alone. I still would have tried, but it was easier with Aaron in my corner.

Felix grabbed the remote and put on some history documentary show. It made eating in silence a little less tense. When everyone had finished, I gathered their plates and then muted the TV.

"Can we talk?" I asked.

"Talk," Felix replied. He folded his arms and glared at me. I wasn't sure if I'd be able to fully fix everything with him in this conversation alone. But I had to start somewhere. I took a deep breath.

"These waffles are my olive branch," I said. "Actually, I've been trying to give you tiny olive branches this whole last week, but this is the Official Big Olive Branch." I paused, taking another deep breath. "Felix, Aaron, Wendy, I am so so so sorry I broke the Oregon Rule. It was shitty of me to do that to all of you, and to keep it all a secret. That was two fuck-ups. And you guys didn't deserve either of them."

Felix leaned forward and rested his elbows on his knees. His face hadn't softened. "Did I ever tell you the full story of why I made the Oregon Rule?" he asked.

I shook my head. He'd instituted it from the very beginning of the Boy Scouts of Atlantis, and it had just seemed like a generally good policy. I didn't know there was an actual story behind it.

"The first band I was ever in," Felix said, "was my sophomore year in college. I had spent my whole life up to that point dreaming about being in a band. It was the only thing that kept me in piano lessons as a little kid. I wanted to be Jerry Lee Lewis. When I was a teenager and just trying to get through high school, I would think about the day when I would be a musician. The first show I ever played with that first band was one of the best days of my life."

There was a softness to Felix's words and voice that I hadn't heard from him before. The man expressed his feelings with his clothes and his music, not with personal stories. I held still, not wanting him to stop.

"I was 19," he said. "And after a few months of playing shows, this girl named Eva joined our group. She was…" Felix stared at the ground. "She was incredible. She had this voice, and I couldn't take my eyes off her when she was onstage. We all went on tour together, just up to Eugene, Oregon and back. And one night after one of the Oregon shows, Eva and I stayed late to pack up gear, and I kissed her. We started hooking up, and we didn't tell anyone for weeks."

I couldn't believe I'd never heard any of this before. Felix and I weren't super close, but it had somehow never occurred to me to ask for details about the Oregon Rule. He'd always just said he had a bad experience while on tour in Oregon and left it at that.

"When the rest of the band finally found out," Felix said, "they went ballistic. One of the other guys had had a crush on her that none of us knew about, and he blamed me for 'stealing his girl' which I told him was misogynist bullshit, because it was. Then someone else said I was only —" Felix stopped and cleared his throat, "I was only fucking Eva because her dad was in the music business, which I swear I didn't know. And it turned out Eva wasn't that serious about me, which hurt a lot to find out. The whole band imploded."

Felix leveled me with his gaze. "Do you get it, Simon? The one thing, the one fucking thing keeping me on earth got shattered. The one thing this awkward, skinny, lonely emo kid had was yanked away because of what I had done. So I swore I would never let something like that ever happen again."

The room was completely silent. I could see so much hurt in Felix's face—all the ache and pain he still carried from that time years ago. My throat felt tight.

Aaron was the first one to speak. "I'm sorry that happened, Felix," he said quietly.

Felix nodded, but he kept his eyes on me. "I want to make sure you understand, Simon. I'm not just a strict asshole for no reason."

"F-Felix," I stammered. "I…I'm so glad you told me… everything. And it makes what I did one thousand times shittier. You shouldn't have had to explain anything about the Oregon Rule for me to take it seriously."

"What I want to know is," Wendy asked, "is why didn't you *tell* us?"

I turned to him. "Because I didn't want to hurt you."

Wendy shook his head. "Not *after* you broke the rule. *Before*. When you were first attracted to Marlowe. We could have talked through it, figured something out."

I stared at him. "That…honestly never even occurred to me," I confessed.

"Dumbass," Wendy said, shaking his head at the ground.

"I deserve that," I said.

"Simon," Felix said. I turned back to him. "You can't ever do shit like this again. If we're gonna keep making music together…damning hell, if we're going to be *friends*, you have to talk to us. You have to say things out loud."

I was having a ridiculous realization. "This is going to sound so dumb, but I think…I think I just assumed that liking someone was also against the Oregon Rule?"

"Dumbass!" Wendy repeated.

"I know!" I replied, throwing my hands into the air.

"But I promise to never do shit like this again. I promise to talk to everyone. I'm so sorry I didn't."

"For sure?" Felix asked, his eyebrows raised.

I looked at him. "For sure," I said. "I um…I don't say this a lot, but you guys mean the world to me. Both as people and as bandmates. I can't believe I ever risked that. I never want to do that again."

Felix searched my face, and then nodded once.

"Are you willing to shake on it?" Wendy asked. I held out my hand, and when Wendy gripped it, he smiled at me. "Truce," he said.

Aaron reached out to shake my hand as well. "I'm already good, dude, but the handshake makes it official."

I looked over at Felix and held out my hand. He looked at it, and then looked up at me. "Are you going to ask Marlowe out when we get home?"

I blinked at him. "I…I want to," I said. "I know there might still be some residual, I dunno, feelings from you guys, and maybe Queen Anne too, but I…I think I love her."

Felix studied me for a full two seconds, and then he reached out and clasped my hand. "Don't keep secrets, Simon. Not from us, and not from her."

And then, despite all my efforts, a single tear escaped my eye, and I swiped it away while gripping Felix's hand as tightly as I could.

CHAPTER 31

But I Won't Do That

AUGUST 20: ALAMEDA, CALIFORNIA

MARLOWE

Getting an ice cream cone was a terrible idea. My vision for this moment was so romantic—I'd be waiting on the pier with an ice cream cone for Simon and one for me, a throwback to the day in the park in Portland. An adorable, Instagram-worthy reunion, the Bay Bridge in the distance. But it was late August and it was completely impossible to keep either ice cream from melting. I decided one of them was a lost cause and threw it away, but it seemed a shame to waste two, so I was desperately trying to eat the second one before it melted.

I was also insanely nervous. Because I wanted to be with Simon and I was trying to figure out the exact right words to use to tell him. I'd come up with about a dozen scripts that were all wrong. I licked a drip of ice cream from the cone in my hand.

"Marlowe!"

I looked up to see Simon striding toward me. And all of my thoughts stopped.

He was wearing a faded Pearl Jam t-shirt and pants that hugged him in all the right places. He had on that green button-up that brought out his eyes, open and rolled up at the sleeves. Converse all-stars. Leather bracelets.

The breeze blew his brown curls away from his face, and when I saw his hazel eyes, my heart lurched. He was smiling at me a little uncertainly.

I was absolutely, completely, hopelessly in love with him. Complete simp, obsessed, stick a fork in me, I was done. He came to a stop in front of me, and I tried not to melt into a puddle.

"Hi," I said.

"Hi." We looked at one another for a moment. Then Simon pointed to my ice cream cone. "I almost got one of those to bring you," he said.

I grinned. "I technically got one for you, too, but it melted too fast." I held out my half-eaten cone. "You can finish this one if you want."

Simon reached out and took the cone from me, then moved his tongue to take a long lick of ice cream. I'm pretty sure my mouth fell open at the sight of it. Oh, to be that ice cream…

"So," Simon said, jolting my thoughts back into place.

"So," I replied. "That was the worst two and a half weeks ever."

Simon laughed gently. "Amen. I hated that."

"But I think it was necessary," I said. I turned and leaned against the pier railing, looking out over the bay. The metal was warm against my forearms. "Music is really important to me," I said. "And so is Queen Anne. My friendships with Ducky and Rose and Jem are…I can't believe I almost lost that." I turned my head to look at Simon. "If I'm going to be with someone, they have to fit into my life alongside music and those friendships. I can't bring myself to sacrifice one for the other. I won't do that."

Simon's eyes searched my face. "So you would do anything for love…"

"But I won't do that," I finished, smiling. I let the word "love" hover in the air between us, not quite ready to address it.

Simon leaned on the pier railing next to me, taking another bite of ice cream. "Felix told me more about why he made the Oregon Rule," he said. "I had never heard the full story, and when I did…" He shook his head. "It was awful, what happened. It made what we did feel ten times worse."

My stomach sank. This suddenly didn't feel like a "let's be together" conversation. This felt like a "I regret every-thing" conversation.

"But Marlowe, I…" Simon looked at me. "Maybe the circumstances were shitty. But I think…shit, I don't know how to say this but to just say it, but I love you."

Fireworks went off in my chest. I wanted to dance. If I knew how to do a back handspring, I would have done a hundred of them.

"I love you," I said. "Oh my god, Simon, I love the hell out of you."

Simon looked a little uncertain. "Like, as a friend, or…?"

"No, like as more than that," I said. "And also as a friend, but I love the hell out of you like, I'm in love with you. I've been standing on this pier, trying to figure out how to tell you."

Simon flung the remains of the ice cream cone into the bay and turned to grab my upper arms. "Marlowe, I'm in love with you," he said. His voice was firm and desperate.

I needed to kiss him or I might die. I leaned in, but

before my lips could meet his, he held me in place. "Wait," he said. "Before we…before we do anything, is this okay with Queen Anne? Like, did you all make up?"

I nodded. "I sang them a John Denver song and then we all cried in the living room," I said. "Are the Boy Scouts all good?"

Simon nodded back. "I made them waffles and we all shook hands."

I smiled. "So then…can we kiss now?"

Simon didn't answer, he just yanked me to his chest and planted his mouth on mine.

My blood rushed through my whole body, sending me onto my tiptoes to reach Simon's lips better. He tilted his head to deepen the kiss, and I couldn't stifle the hungry noise that came out of my throat. Suddenly, Simon's hands gripped my hips and pressed me back against the railing, kissing me harder. His lips moved down the side of my neck, his nose brushing my skin.

"Simon?" I gasped.

"Mmmm?"

"Do you want to come over?"

Simon lifted his head to look at me, his pupils wide, his cheeks flushed. "Yes," he said.

Simon and I each took our separate cars and got to my place at almost the exact same time. We both practically sprinted to the front door. Rose and Jem and Ducky were all out, but I don't think I would have cared. I hauled Simon down the hallway to my bedroom, slammed the door, and shoved him onto my bed.

He was already pulling his button-up and t-shirt off by

the time I crawled up his body. I straddled his hips and leaned down to kiss him.

Holy shit, Simon was in my bed, and we were making out, and we would get to keep doing this all the time??? I dragged my palms down his chest, hooking my fingers into his pants.

"Fucking hell, Marlowe," he gritted out. His hands made their way to my tits, cupping them roughly. My eyes fluttered closed.

"Wait, I can't take my clothes off if you're doing that," I stammered.

"I'll help you," Simon replied. He sat up to lift my shirt over my head. His fingers brushing my skin as he unhooked my bra felt like a form of worship. He laid me back on the bed, unbuttoning, unzipping, sliding fabric off of me. When I was bare before him, he sat and just looked at me for a moment. I felt suddenly shy.

"What?" I asked.

"I'm just wondering how the hell I got so lucky," Simon said. I grinned and pulled him down on top of me, reaching down to undo his pants. I shoved them down over his hips, revealing how hard he was for me.

"I'm kind of obsessed with your body," I said. I reached out to wrap my hand around his cock, and Simon let out a groan. I pumped him once. "And you," I added.

Simon tilted his hips into my fist, his arms braced on either side of my head. "I'll...compliment you back... when I can think straight," he said.

I let go of him so that I could pull him down onto me, chest against chest, hip to hip. My legs fell open to make room for him. My lips found his again, his tongue moving into my mouth.

Simon kissed down my throat, between my breasts, in a

line down my stomach. My breath hitched as I realized where he was heading.

The heat of his mouth on my most sensitive spot was torture and ecstasy all at once. I arched into the sensation, reaching down to grasp handfuls of his hair. He growled in approval.

His lips and tongue worked me until I was squirming against the mattress, until I was gripping handfuls of the sheets to try and brace myself, until I was actually and literally screaming his name.

My orgasm moved through me, wave after wave of pleasure pulsing in my blood until I was gasping for breath. When I finally looked down, Simon was staring up at me, a heated look in his eyes.

CHAPTER 32
The Right Rules
AUGUST 20: ALAMEDA, CALIFORNIA

SIMON

For as long as I lived, I would never get tired of watching Marlowe come. Everything from the sounds she made to the way her lips moved to the glow of her skin was so fucking perfect. She looked down at me, her chest still heaving.

"Simon," she said. Her voice was part wonder, part adoration.

I crawled up her body and settled my hips between her thighs, brushing my hardness up against where I wanted to be most. I was instantly coated in Marlowe's arousal, and it practically made my eyes roll back in my head. "Fuck, you're wet," I groaned.

"It's you," Marlowe whispered. Then she reached over to her nightstand drawer and pulled out a condom. I rolled it on and a few seconds later, I sank into her, feeling her body wrap around me, taking me in. I drew my hips back and then thrust forward again, driving Marlowe's body up the mattress slightly.

"Hold on to me, sweetheart," I said. She gripped my ribs with her hands. "Closer," I told her. I drew her arms up around my neck and then pulled her close to me, wrapping my arms around her, bringing our bodies flush. I started moving faster, getting closer to my release.

Marlowe let out a string of curse words and clenched around me, and suddenly I was even more in love with her than I was two minutes ago. She gripped the back of my head, making those incredible sounds as I moved inside of her. I dropped my lips to hers as if I could swallow every noise she made. She was perfect. I pulled away just enough to look into her face.

Her blue eyes looked right into the very heart of me, filling me up, bringing me home. She held my gaze as my climax tore through me, my hips thrusting hard, my breathing tightening into a moan. I collapsed to one side of her, my head resting on one of her breasts.

After spending the next few minutes—or maybe hours?—in a glorious post-sex haze, I lifted my head to look at Marlowe.

"Hi," I said.

"Hi," she smiled.

"I kind of want to stay here forever." I nuzzled my face into her neck and then down to the softness of her breasts.

"I also want you to stay here forever," Marlowe replied. She ran a hand through my hair.

"We do have to pause the afterglow to clean up," I said. It was literal torture to lift myself off her bed and make my way to the attached bathroom. Once the condom was taken care of, I climbed back into Marlowe's bed and drew her into my arms. I heard her give a soft chuckle.

"What?" I asked.

"I'm just thinking about how I'm the luckiest girl alive," she said. She gazed up at me. "You're my *boyfriend*."

A question moved over her face. "Wait. You are my boyfriend, right?"

"I am absolutely your boyfriend," I said.

"Oh thank god." Marlowe settled back down. "That gives me the right to fight off all the groupies trying to fuck you at shows."

"There aren't groupies trying to fuck me at my shows!" I protested.

"Oh yes, there are," Marlowe said. "You're just oblivious."

Huh. If that was true, I was vaguely flattered, even if Marlowe was teasing. I squeezed her to me and kissed the side of her head. "You're the only groupie I care about."

Marlowe made an indignant noise and sat up. "Excuse me, how do you know *you're* not the groupie in this situation?!"

I smiled up at her, then reached out to run a hand from her neck to her belly. "Oh, I'm definitely the groupie in this situation."

Marlowe smiled and returned to her spot in my arms.

"I think we should make some rules that we can actually follow," Marlowe said.

My stomach gave a tiny lurch. Was she going to propose a groupie hall pass situation or something? Because I was not interested in anything but being with her. "Like what?"

"Like…first of all, exclusivity," Marlowe said. "I want you and nothin' but you."

I felt a rush of relief. "Oh thank you baby Jesus," I said, tightening my hold on her. "That's also what I want. Oh my god I like you so much. And love you so much."

She lifted her face to kiss me. "I also like and love you so much."

I felt like there was an entire sunrise glowing in my

chest. I half expected light to start shooting out of my fingertips or something. I was holding a miracle of a dream girl in my arms, and she wanted to be my girlfriend. She liked *and* loved me.

I turned us so that she was on her back and attacked her face with kisses. Marlowe laughed and mock struggled. "Oh no!" she said. "Help! I'm being adored!"

I laughed and laid back down beside her. We both turned onto our sides so that we were facing each other. "I hope kiss attacks are not against the rules," I said. "Because my adoration cannot be controlled."

Marlowe gripped both sides of my face and squeezed. "Why are you so *cute*!?" she demanded.

I opened my mouth to give her some kind of flirtatious answer, but she clamped a hand over my mouth.

"Wait, stop being cute for a second, because I have one more rule suggestion and you're distracting me."

I nodded, and then Marlowe removed her hand. She sat up and looked toward her bedroom door for a second, then looked back at me. "Music is really important to me," she said. "And so are my friendships. If ever this…us… comes between me and those things, we need to…re-evaluate. Or something. I don't think it will, but I wanted to say it out loud. At the beginning. The rule is that friendship and music are equally as important as this relationship. Not more or less important. The same amount important. Can you…is that okay?"

I sat up so that we were across from each other. "Your love of music and your love of your friends are part of why I fell so hard for you," I said. I reached out to cup her face in one hand. "I can't imagine loving you any other way. If ever I were to dim either of those things, I wouldn't deserve you." To my surprise, Marlowe's eyes shone with tears. "Oh, sweetheart!" I exclaimed.

"I fucking love you," she said. She lifted a hand to cover mine on her face. "So much."

"I fucking love *you* so much," I replied. I searched her face for a moment. "I have a suggestion for another rule."

Marlowe nodded. "Rule of threes, I like it."

I smiled. "I say that the third rule is that we re-examine the rules every now and then. The Oregon Rule had good reasons behind it, but…but if we had all just talked about what we were feeling, if we had trusted ourselves and each other better, we could have saved ourselves and everyone else a lot of heartache. But I just didn't think to question the Oregon Rule. I don't think to question any rules, really."

"And I question all of them," Marlowe grinned.

"Exactly," I said. "I think the exclusivity rule and the music and friendship being equal to the relationship rule are both great, and honestly I can't see us changing them. But it might be worth it to just check in now and then. To look at why we have the rules and how well they're still serving us and why."

Marlowe smiled at me. "This is the hottest you've ever been," she said.

"You're just saying that because I'm naked."

"I'm saying that because I'm in love with you," she grinned. "And I say yes to all of those rules, including the rule about questioning rules."

And then I couldn't stop myself from kissing her again.

$$Six\ months\ later$$

FEBRUARY 14: ALAMEDA, CALIFORNIA
MARLOWE

I still had not gotten over how hot Simon was onstage. I liked to think the feeling was mutual, because sometimes when I put my foot up on the monitor to solo, and I caught his eye in the audience, he looked like he wanted to eat me. Earlier tonight, he fully bit his lip while watching me play.

I looked up at him onstage now, his fingers flying over the frets in a way that was truly impressive. He glanced back at Felix, who gave him a rare grin as he picked up the melody of "Third Grade Throw Down." Then Simon turned to the mic and screamed into it, his jaw tight, his curly hair hanging around his face, his forearms on full display.

Ducky leaned over to me. "Do you ever look up at that and think 'holy shit that's my boyfriend'?"

"All the time," I replied, not taking my eyes off of Simon.

The boys were reaching the chaotic climax of the song, Wendy practically throwing his drumsticks around but still somehow managing to be perfectly on beat. Aaron just smiling at everyone like the lovable golden retriever he was. Felix banging on the keys of his keyboard and Simon was swinging his guitar around as he played. One last perfect chord and the crowd erupted into cheers.

Simon smiled at everyone, then spoke into the mic. "I wrote this next song for my girlfriend before she was my girlfriend," he said. He looked down and winked at me, then turned back to the crowd. "Life lesson: don't keep your love interests secret from your friends. That's not what this song is about, but I felt like you should know."

He launched into the haunting opening notes of "Siren," and I let those familiar, devastatingly sexy words wash over me.

Her siren song
I'm all at sea
She's calling me
I know it's wrong
My sailor's thoughts
All tied in knots

I didn't think I would ever get over the fact that the hottest song I had ever heard had been written about *me*. I moved my hips to the music, closing my eyes to get lost in it. Simon was gonna get all kinds of laid tonight.

When the song finished, Simon addressed the crowd again. "And now I'd like to invite my girlfriend and the rest of Queen Anne back up onstage, to sing a little song we like to call 'The Trees Here Are Too Fucking Big.'"

Ducky hauled herself up the front of the stage and grabbed her tambourine from next to the drums, and Rose carried her bass onstage. Jem and I took our usual places at the mics.

"Hey Jem, you wanna tell them about this song?" Simon asked.

Jem turned to address the crowd. "So, last summer, the Boy Scouts of Atlantis and Queen Anne did a west coast tour. We stopped at Redwood National Forest, and the trees there are really fucking big. So we wrote a dumb song about it around the campfire, and then we played it on the rest of the tour."

"And found love along the way!" Ducky added.

Aaron stepped up to the mic and bent down to speak into it. "Maybe the real love is the friendships we made along the way."

Simon grinned at him. "That's the most true thing you've ever said." He played the opening chords of the trees song, the familiar D, D major seven, D seven pattern, and we all launched into our beloved trees song.

It had taken us a minute to bring it back. Our bands had played half a dozen shows together in the last six months, and the first few times, we had skipped the trees song. It still felt a little tender somehow…like all of the memories of the west coast tour were still colored by the hurt from the last few days of it. Like there was still a bruise there that needed to heal. But the more time went on, the more Simon and I fit into each other's lives, the more time Queen Anne and the Boy Scouts spent together, the more we fell back into the camaraderie of last summer. When we did finally bring the trees song back into performances, we all grinned the whole time. It had felt like a reunion.

I leaned into the mic, my mouth close to Simon's, as we sang the chorus. "The trees here are too fucking big, the trees here are too fucking big!" Simon leaned forward a little to yell at the crowd, "Sing along!" The audience joined us in the refrain. Ducky was going ham on the tambourine, and Aaron and Rose were facing each other, doing competing bass lines. I knew that if I looked back, I'd see Felix playing the keyboard with a tiny hint of a smile on his face, and Wendy looking like a maniac, in contrast to his ethereal warmth offstage.

I caught Simon's eye, and my heart swelled with so much gratitude. I got to have three of my favorite things: music, my friends, and Simon. And sometimes I got to have them all simultaneously, like this moment onstage. I didn't think I could smile any wider—my joy was too big.

When the song ended, Simon swung his guitar around to his back and wrapped an arm around my waist. He pulled me to him and kissed me. I could hear a few wolf whistles from the crowd. When Simon pulled away, he just looked at me. "I'm so stupid in love with you, Marlowe," he said, shouting over the cheers from the crowd.

"I am stupid in love with you, Simon," I replied, then took his face in my hands and stood on tiptoe to kiss him again.

Get a sneak peek at the next book in the series!

What's a kiss or two between friends?

Read Felix and Rose's story in
Kisses Worth Waiting For

Kisses Worth Waiting For

"I couldn't even like, adjust my mouth to the kiss size," Simon said, his arm around Marlowe. "She was like…it was like she was going to the dentist. Like, AAAAHHH-HH." Ducky collapsed on the floor in laughter, her purple hair covering her face.

Marlowe grinned at her boyfriend. "I think you might win the Most Awkward First Kiss award."

"I don't even know if you can count it as a kiss," Simon said. His hazel eyes danced while he played with Marlowe's long brown hair. "It was a…mouth mauling."

"My first kiss was sweet," Marlowe said, leaning into Simon. "The most tiny, chaste peck after a school dance. I've gotten better at kissing since then."

"Yeah, you have," Simon grinned.

Ducky sat up. "Will you two stop being adorable? Okay. Rose's turn. Tell us your first kiss story."

My cheeks grew hot. I turned back to the cactus plants

near the window I was watering, trying to decide if I wanted to make something up to spare myself the embarrassment or be honest. The honesty route was painful, but I didn't think I'd be capable of coming up with a good enough lie.

"I um…" I murmured.

"Come on," Marlowe said. "It can't be that bad."

I turned to see four pairs of eyes staring at me. Simon and Marlowe from the couch, Ducky from the floor, Felix from the armchair that had become "his" after the last year of coming over.

"I've never been kissed," I mumbled. Barely loud enough to be heard.

"What?" Ducky asked.

"I said I've never been kissed!" I yelled.

The room was silent.

"No, I heard what you said, I'm just surprised," Ducky said.

"Never?" Marlowe asked.

I put down the watering can and shook my head.

"This is a very personal question, but are you ace?" Ducky asked. "Like, asexual?"

"Definitely not," I replied.

Ducky studied my face. "Do you want to be kissed?"

"Of course I want to be kissed!" I exclaimed. I was still embarrassed, but Ducky's questions were opening something up in me. "I'm twenty-four years old! I've wanted to be kissed for like, a decade! Longer!"

Another beat of silence.

"I mean," Marlowe said. "I don't blame you. Kissing is awesome."

"I highly recommend it," Simon added, pressing his lips to Marlowe's cheekbone.

Ducky rolled her eyes, "Oh my god, we know. You're into each other."

My stomach rolled. It's not that I was jealous of Marlowe exactly…I had zero feelings for Simon outside of friendship. He was like a big brother to me. It was that I wanted what she had.

Just…with someone else.

I was very happy for Marlowe and Simon, truly. But my loneliness had grown heavier over the past year. There was so much joy in our house now, even more than there was before, with Simon and the other boys coming over all the time. I was grateful. But my patient heart ached sometimes.

Ducky's voice snapped me back to the present. "I'm asking you this like, practically," she said. "Not just desire-wise. Do you want to be kissed?"

I blinked at her. "Are you…offering? Because I'm not gay. Or bi."

"No, I'm not offering, although I would be honored. Even though I'm also not gay. Or bi. I'm saying if you want to be kissed, then let's get you kissed!"

"But…how?" I asked.

Ducky shrugged. "We've got tons of options. Tinder, a groupie at a show…"

"Don't be a bad influence," Marlowe said.

Ducky glared at her. "Are you slut-shaming me?"

Marlowe pressed her lips into a thin line and looked thoughtful. "Actually, I think maybe I was? Sorry. That was shitty."

Simon gathered her up into his arms. "My account-ability queen!"

"You're forgiven," Ducky said. She turned her attention back to me. "I'm obviously not going to do anything without your consent. But I'm just saying, if you want to be kissed, I will absolutely help make that happen."

"I'd feel…weird," I said. "If it was a stranger. It doesn't have to be like a 'Disney true love kiss,' but I don't think I could just kiss anyone."

Ducky nodded. "It needs to be someone you know."

"I'll do it."

My eyes snapped to Felix. He was sitting in his usual chair, in his usual all-black attire. He didn't even look up as he spoke—he was scrolling his phone. When the room went quiet, he looked up at all of us. Even after all these years, there were still startling moments when his green eyes sent electricity through me. When his features took me by surprise.

I could hardly breathe.

Ducky broke the silence. "That…might actually be perfect?"

Simon sat up on the couch. "Wait a minute, what about the Oregon Rule?"

The Oregon Rule stated that no one should date or hook up with anyone you're in a band with or on tour with. Which was the cause of a lot of heartache when Simon and Marlowe first got together, but we'd kept the rule in place anyway. They were the only exception.

Felix shrugged. "You two have been dating for a year, and we've all been fine. Besides, it's not like Rose and I would start dating. It's just a kiss."

My blood was on fire. For so many reasons. Because Felix was talking about kissing me. Because he was saying we *wouldn't* start dating. Because *the boy I'd loved since high school was talking about kissing me.*

Marlowe leaned forward. "Wait, but that was before we formed Queenscout. We're all literally in a band together now. All the Boy Scouts of Atlantis and all of Queen Anne."

Ducky leaned back, resting on her hands. "Yeah, but the Oregon Rule is 'no dating or hooking up with people in the same band or a band you're on tour with.' It doesn't say anything about 'a friend kissing another friend as a favor.'"

Felix stood and stretched. I glanced away from the thin strip of skin I could see when his t-shirt lifted. "Exactly." He looked over at me, and I felt my skin flush. He searched my face. "But if Rose doesn't want to, that's fine. I'm just offering as a friend. I'm going home. Are you coming?"

I sat frozen. For the last year, as Felix had gotten into the habit of coming over, I'd gotten into the habit of walking him home. Those ten minute walks were precious to me, but now this one felt loaded. Anything could happen on a walk. And everyone in the room knew it.

I debated with myself for a moment. I didn't want to lose our walks, now or ever, because of some kind of awkwardness. But I didn't want to deal with everyone else's awkwardness if I stayed here. Finally, I nodded and stood, feeling faint. I was grateful that Marlowe, Ducky, and Simon didn't make a big deal out of my walking home with Felix, after the conversation we had all just had.

I felt unsteady on my feet as Felix and I walked the few blocks to the apartment he shared with his bandmates. His offer to kiss me was ping pong-ing through my whole body. I couldn't think about anything else. But Felix was his usual serious self.

When we got to his place, he stopped on the sidewalk.

We never stopped on the sidewalk.

"Rose," Felix said. I lifted my gaze to his.

"Yeah?"

"Are you okay?"

I nodded. "Yeah," I said. "Just…yes."

"I didn't mean to make things weird," Felix said.

"You didn't!" I exclaimed. Even though he most certainly did. But I didn't want him to feel bad about it. "*I'm* just weird. It's me. Like, you didn't make things weird, they were just weird to begin with. Because I'm weird."

Any other boy might have tried to contradict me, but Felix just shrugged. "The offer still stands," he said. "If you just want to try kissing with someone with no stakes or whatever. Just to get it out of the way."

I could kiss Felix. He could kiss me. It could even happen right now, here on this cracked sidewalk, if I wanted it to. After years of trying to shove down every daydream I'd ever had about it, it could actually happen.

Kind of.

It was like being told I could hold a star, but only for a second. Unwrapping a Christmas present that was meant for someone else. It would be a shadow of what I actually wanted.

But if I could never have the real thing, maybe a shadow would be enough.

I swallowed. "Can I think about it?"

"Sure," Felix said. "I'm not worried about fucking up our friendship either way."

"Yeah," I said.

"Don't look so freaked out," Felix said, a hint of a smile in his voice. "It would just be a kiss. It's not like we're in love or anything."

"Right," I said.

Then I watched him walk into his apartment and close the door.

～

KISSES WORTH WAITING FOR

AVAILABLE ON KINDLE UNLIMITED, AMAZON, BOOKSHOP.ORG, AND ON ORDER THROUGH YOUR FAVORITE LOCAL INDIE BOOKSTORE

OCTOBER 2025

Acknowledgments

First of all, thank you, dear reader, for picking up this book. You bring each story to life, and I'm forever indebted.

Thank you to the incredible beta readers who took the time to read early drafts of this book and offered invaluable feedback, specifically Andy Hansen, Sara Goldberg-McRae, Sam Baird, Lindsay Marriott, and Elliott Croft. Special thank you to Ellie Otis, for copy editing work.

Mad thanks to the friends who contributed song names for the imaginary bands of Queen Anne and The Boy Scouts of Atlantis: Taylor Jack Nelson, Kim Hawker, Sofia Kendrick Paredes, Dava Tuttle, and Andrew Pincock.

Shout out to the following Salt Lake/Provo music scene folks, for putting on killer shows and making killer music, especially Queenadilla, Derm, Dosey Don't, The By and By, Cinderbiter, Auhre, Homestyle Dinner Rolls, Chi Chi Le Mot, and Little Moon. (Everyone go check them out on Spotify, iTunes, Apple Music, YouTube, BandCamp, etc.)

Additional shout out to all of the Salt Lake/Provo music venues, whose lit stages and weird bathrooms hold a special place in my heart: Kilby Court, Urban Lounge, ABG's Bar, Velour, Metro Music Hall, The Rise, Center of the Universe, The Depot, and all of the living rooms and back yards where people put on shows.

So much love to the Deep Love Rock Opera (found) family, whose friendship and love of music inspired so much of this book. Current and past members of this ghoulish little group are forever in my heart. Times we've spent at shows and on the road together are precious to me, and so much of this story wouldn't be on the page if it weren't for you all.

Special thanks to Chase McKnight for writing an initial version of Simon's "Siren" song, even though I changed all of the lyrics and you guys didn't end up using the song on Queenadilla's new album.

I am forever indebted to the Facebook groups 20Books-to50K, The Writing Gals, The Writing Gals Critique Group, and Romance Writers Support League.

This one might be weird but honestly thanks to the Roadtrippers.com website, for helping me map out this tour (even though you didn't remind me that my annual subscription was renewing and charged me $35.99 for something I didn't need anymore).

Thank you to Oma, whose generous financial support allowed me to pour more time, energy, and resources into writing than I would have had otherwise.

Shout out to my ride-or-die Mikah, for their endless encouragement and for giving both Simon and Felix their names.

Love to all of the women and femmes in my life who read and love romance novels, with special love to Brittany and Lily. Your quiet and sometimes not-so-quiet sisterhood sustains me more than you know.

And finally, thank you to these characters, who revealed themselves to me slowly and beautifully, and allowed me to both live out my own quiet rock star dreams and celebrate my real life loud gratitude for friendship.

Also by Elle Whittaker

WEST TINDALE

Halfway to You (August 2025)

Halfway Across the Street (September 2025)

Halfway Through the Holidays

ROCK ROMANCE

Kisses Worth Waiting For (October 2025)

ENCOUNTERS

Under His Hands

At Your Service

OTHER THINGS

Jane Eyre and Zombies

About the Author

Elle Whittaker is the pen name for Liz Whittaker, who is the daughter of a poem and an ancient Egyptian hieroglyph. She spent most of her time on the shores of Neverland before moving to Salt Lake City, where she currently lives in a library until she can afford an RV. Her heart alternates between pumping lemonade and ink. Her favorite foods are music and knowledge, which she eats as often as possible from atop her mountain of crippling student debt. Her other job is theatre. In her free time, she enjoys hugging trees, cross-stitching, and thinking about outer space. She is happily a victim of the kind of moonstruck madness that drives her to not only write romance novels, but poetry, scripts, essays, and theatre reviews under various names.

instagram.com/ellewhittakerromance

tiktok.com/@elle.whittaker.romance